Michael Underwood and The Murder Room

〉〉〉 This title is part of The Murder Room, our series dedicated to making available out-of-print or hard-to-find titles by classic crime writers.

Crime fiction has always held up a mirror to society. The Victorians were fascinated by sensational murder and the emerging science of detection; now we are obsessed with the forensic detail of violent death. And no other genre has so captivated and enthralled readers.

Vast troves of classic crime writing have for a long time been unavailable to all but the most dedicated frequenters of second-hand bookshops. The advent of digital publishing means that we are now able to bring you the backlists of a huge range of titles by classic and contemporary crime writers, some of which have been out of print for decades.

From the genteel amateur private eyes of the Golden Age and the femmes fatales of pulp fiction, to the morally ambiguous hard-boiled detectives of mid twentieth-century America and their descendants who walk our twenty-first century streets, The Murder Room has it all. **〉〉〉**

The Murder Room
Where Criminal Minds Meet

themurderroom.com

Michael Underwood (1916–1992)
Michael Underwood (the pseudonym of John Michael Evelyn) was born in Worthing, Sussex and educated at Christ Church College, Oxford. He was called to the Bar in 1939 and served in the British army during World War Two. He returned to work in the Department of Public Prosecutions until his retirement in 1976, and wrote almost 50 crime novels informed by his career in the law. His five series characters include Sergeant Nick Atwell and lawyer Rosa Epton, of whom is was said by the *Washington Post* that she 'outdoes Perry Mason'.

A Crime Apart

Michael Underwood

An Orion book

Copyright © Isobel Mackenzie 1966

The right of Michael Underwood to be identified as the author of this work has been asserted in accordance with the Copyright, Designs and Patents Act 1988.

This edition published by
The Orion Publishing Group Ltd
Orion House
5 Upper St Martin's Lane
London WC2H 9EA

An Hachette UK company
A CIP catalogue record for this book is available from the British Library

ISBN 978 1 4719 0806 4

www.orionbooks.co.uk

I

LONG before the car came to a halt in front of the trim bungalow, with its small apron of lawn bordered by some now rather straggling lupins and wall-flowers, Miss Frayne had gathered her belongings on to her lap and was holding her front-door key like a talisman in her right hand.

"Don't bother to get out, dear," she said to her nephew, Ted, as the car drew up. "I can manage."

He leaned across to open the passenger door. "It really was awfully good of you to come and look after the children this weekend, Aunt Sylvia. We could never have left them but for you. There's no need to tell you how grateful we are."

"I'm sure it did you both a world of good to have a weekend away from them," Miss Frayne replied, her tone conveying nothing of the drained energy which forty-eight hours of looking after her six-year-old great-niece and four-year-old great-nephew had cost her. She'd sooner weed the garden any day and secretly hoped she wouldn't be called to duty again too soon.

Duty was, however, the keynote of her life. Duty toward her family, toward the community in which she lived: duty, even, toward her next-door neighbour, Mrs. Hibbert, who, heaven knew, was able to tax to the uttermost the most Christian sense of duty.

"Good-night, Ted," Miss Frayne called out, as the Ford Cortina spurted away from the kerb. "Give my love to Judy." An unnecessary injunction since Miss Frayne had only fifteen minutes previously kissed the lady in question good-bye and would almost certainly be seeing her again before the week was out. Indeed, she would be spending the forthcoming Wednesday evening at her nephew's house as she had spent each Wednesday over the past four years.

1

For several seconds after she had got out of the car, Miss Frayne stood on the pavement, gazing with quiet proprietary pleasure at her home. It was certainly good to be back after two nights in a strange bed. The church clock was striking the half-hour as she marched up the short path. She'd be just in time to listen to community hymn singing which was her favourite Sunday evening radio programme. As she inserted her front-door key in the lock, she glanced instinctively at Mrs. Hibbert's house next door, which had been built at a period when houses made up in solidity what their design lacked in imagination and furthermore whose interior reflected comfort rather than taste. Certainly no one could have charged Mr. Hibbert, who had died ten years previously, and who had been a master builder, with any architectural flights of imagination. His memorial, in the shape of settlements of worthy suburban homes, would continue to stand defiantly against an engulfing tide of weird glass and concrete structures for many a year to come.

At this particular moment, however, Miss Frayne's attention was not attracted by the complacently solid appearance of her neighbour's house but by the presence of Nero, Mrs. Hibbert's large, pampered, black cat, sitting in obvious dudgeon on the side doorstep.

"What are you doing there, Nero?" Miss Frayne demanded, puzzled by the unexpected sight. It wasn't that it was late, simply that Nero always stayed indoors after his supper at six o'clock until his evening prowl at ten-thirty, which was half an hour before Mrs. Hibbert retired to bed. And Miss Frayne had long regarded her neighbour and her neighbour's cat as as much creatures of habit as she was herself. People who lived alone often became so, particularly elderly ladies with large black cats. The fact that Mrs. Hibbert also had a lodger didn't destroy the image for Miss Frayne, since each so obviously went her own way. But then Miss Frayne remembered that Peggy Dunkley, the lodger, had left suddenly two days before. On the Friday, that was. In some way she couldn't have explained, this now remembered detail accounted satisfactorily for the present lapse in routine. Nevertheless, she walked over to the dividing fence and in a winning tone called out Nero's name. But the animal only cast her a disdainful glance and looked away, and Miss Frayne went inside her own house and soon forgot about him in the pleasure of being home again.

The first thing she always did on waking each morning was to go downstairs and make a cup of tea. She was one of those people who are not only brightly alert as soon as their eyes open, but who are tiresomely fond of proclaiming this as some kind of virtue.

While she was waiting for the kettle to boil on Monday morning, she went from window to window drawing back the curtains and satisfying herself that everything was as it should be with her neighbours. She was relieved to observe no sign of Nero, which meant that normal routine had been resumed next door and no activity need be expected for another hour when Mrs. Hibbert would come downstairs to collect her newspaper and give Nero his breakfast saucer of milk. After that, he would appear in the garden, though his mistress wouldn't be seen until around eleven o'clock.

Miss Frayne had just made the tea and was on the point of carrying the tray upstairs when she almost dropped it in alarm as Nero sprang apparently from nowhere on to the window ledge and stared imperiously at her through the glass.

"My dear cat," she murmured, while regaining her composure. "You did give me a start. I'm not used to such early morning visitations. What do you think you're up to?"

Talking to the animal had the effect of reducing her sense of surprise, which was rapidly replaced by one of doubt as to what she should do. Nero's presence on her kitchen window ledge at seven-thirty on a Monday morning was so far removed from routine that some action was clearly called for. But what!

Like the U.N., most governments and all committees, Miss Frayne decided to shelve a decision. Picking up the tray, she addressed herself to Nero through the glass. "If you're still there when I come down, I'll find out what you want."

When forty minutes later she returned to the kitchen, the cat was still waiting, and no sooner had she opened the door than he stalked in. Miss Frayne had nothing to offer him save milk, and this he lapped up as soon as she placed the saucer on the floor and as quickly disposed of a second saucerful.

"You're hungry," she remarked, while wondering what to do next. Everything would have been much easier if she and Mrs. Hibbert enjoyed the neighbourly relations which Miss Frayne had wished to cultivate. But they didn't, though this was not Miss Frayne's fault, since Mrs. Hibbert spared little time for any of her neighbours and invariably brushed aside the proffered hand of friendship with brusque indifference. This, however, was obviously an occasion when neighbourly sense of duty demanded an initiative to be essayed once more. So decided, Miss Frayne's imagination lost no time in conjuring up a scene in which Mrs. Hibbert would display her gratitude in an atmosphere of touching reconciliation. The imagination which produced this happy finale completely failed, however, to disclose any of the circumstances leading up to it.

Leaving Nero still crouched over the saucer of milk, replenished yet a third time, Miss Frayne hurried round to Mrs. Hibbert's front door and bracing herself against whatever might ensue pressed the bell. She found herself torn between the hope that the door would be suddenly opened to reveal a familiar Mrs. Hibbert in a sweater and a pair of too tight slacks, with her badly dyed auburn hair and crudely applied make-up, and that there would be no answer at all. The one would satisfy her sense of duty, even though exposing her to some acid ridicule: the other must inevitably mean yet another decision.

A few minutes later, the matter was placed beyond doubt. The front-door had remained unanswered and an examination of the outside of the house showed it to be completely shut up. With Nero shut out!

Miss Frayne hastened across to Mr. Wimbush who lived opposite and with whom she was on the most neighbourly of terms. The inhabitants of Cresta Drive regarded themselves as a cut above the rest of the neighbourhood. Their houses were all detached (sometimes only just) and were not all alike, and were occupied, for the most part, by retired officials or by ladies with small private incomes like Miss Frayne. She had scarcely taken her hand off the knocker before the door was opened by Mr. Wimbush wearing his dressing-gown and holding a piece of toast and marmalade in one hand.

"Hello, Miss F. Forgive the appearance. Overslept this morning, I'm afraid,"

She waved aside his apology and came immediately to the point. "I'm worried about Mrs. Hibbert."

"Mrs. H.? What's up with her then?"

"She seems to have disappeared. I can't get any answer and Nero's been shut out all night."

"Perhaps she's gone away for the weekend and not told anyone." His expression brightened. "Well, she wouldn't tell anyone would she, not Mrs. H.!"

Miss Frayne clearly didn't regard the suggestion as helpful. "I agree I wouldn't have expected her to tell anybody if she'd gone away, but she certainly wouldn't have left Nero uncared for."

"Blasted cat! Did I tell you how he scratched up the seedlings I'd just sown last week. I'm pretty sure it must have been him." He became aware of Miss Frayne's impatient expression. "Well, I don't quite know what we should do," he added quickly, making a vague gesture with the piece of toast. "I mean there's not a great deal we can do. After all," he concluded lamely, "it's not really any of our business, is it?"

Miss Frayne now registered her irritation. She had turned to someone whom she regarded as staunch and competent as only a retired civil servant could be (Mr. Wimbush had held a minor post in the Ministry of Transport) only to be met by a stream of waffling irrelevance.

"I would certainly regard it as my business if my next-door neighbour was lying stricken in her house and I failed to do anything to help her."

"Ah, but that's the whole point, Miss F.! Is she lying stricken, as you say? Supposing she has gone away for the weekend, supposing she did leave a window open for that great black pest of hers to get in and out and it's accidently shut. . . . See?"

Miss Frayne appeared to ponder this interesting piece of supposition and Mr. Wimbush, who felt he had regained the initiative, decided to press home his advantage.

"I mean one doesn't want to raise all sorts of hares and make a fool of oneself, does one? And anyway what exactly were you proposing to do?"

"Notify the police."

"The police?"

"Who else!"

Mr. Wimbush frowned. "Then, if I may say so, Miss F., I think you should be doubly sure before you do anything so drastic. I doubt whether Mrs. Hibbert would be very pleased to find that you had unleashed the forces of law and order all over her property. Furthermore, what would the neighbours think?" His tongue flicked out like a lizard's to retrieve a shred of marmalade from the edge of his lower lip. "No," he went on, shaking his head to add emphasis to his words, "I think we want to be very certain before we involve the police."

"Well, how long before you consider we *can* be certain?" Miss Frayne asked stubbornly.

Mr. Wimbush had foreseen this question but been hoping it wouldn't be asked. He quite liked Miss Frayne and was always ready to pass a sunny word with any of his neighbours, which meant, in practice, telling them about his garden or regaling them with a chosen reminiscence from his life in the Ministry of Transport, but he had no desire to become involved in any of their problems. This had been Miss Frayne's error, to imagine that his sense of duty would be the equal of her own. It was nothing of the sort. He desired only to be left in peace or to emerge on his own terms.

"We had better wait and see how things develop, hadn't we?" he murmured.

"All right, I'll give it till lunchtime. But if there's no sign of Mrs. Hibbert by then, I shall ring the police." Miss Frayne's tone held a note of irrevocable decision and Mr. Wimbush contented himself with a sage nod.

"I think that would be best," he said, as though the idea had all along been his. With his smoothest departmental approach he went on, "I wouldn't have advocated the more cautious approach, but for the fact that Mrs. Hibbert's lodger . . . what's her name . . . yes, Miss Dunkley . . . that Miss Dunkley left on Friday. And that means Mrs. Hibbert would have been free to go away for the weekend. Before, it wasn't so easy for her."

"If you really want to know," Miss Frayne said pityingly, "Peggy Dunkley didn't present any tie. It was Nero."

"Doubtless you know more about the household than I, Miss F.," Mr. Wimbush's tone was almost offensively bland. The fact was he was getting tired of standing on his doorstep in his dressing-gown and with his breakfast half-consumed. He felt he had given the problem enough of his attention.

Miss Frayne, the impetus of her sense of duty temporarily blurred, returned across the road to her own home to find Nero curled up asleep on one of her best chairs. It occurred to her only then that she hadn't enquired – and Mr. Wimbush had not volunteered – when he had last seen Mrs. Hibbert. Well, there would be time enough for that question later, if need be.

Miss Frayne always spent Monday mornings in her kitchen, doing the week's washing, so it was no hardship to keep a watch on Mrs. Hibbert's house. She also knew that it was her neighbour's custom on Mondays to have an early lunch and then leave the house around half-past twelve to attend the first showing of the new picture at the Regal.

But half-past twelve came and went without any sign of Mrs. Hibbert and on the stroke of one o'clock Miss Frayne picked up the telephone receiver and dialled the number of the local police station, which happened to be one of the furthest flung within the Metropolitan Police District.

"Elwick Common Police Station," a hesitant voice answered at the other end. In fact it was the voice of Police Cadet Temple who lacked assurance only in operating the station switchboard.

"I want to report something," Miss Frayne said boldly.

"What sort of something? A burglary? A lost cat? If you can just give me an idea."

"It concerns my neighbour. I think something may have happened to her."

Police Cadet Temple, who could curb his tendency to facetiousness when he tried very hard, realised from Miss Frayne's tone that this was something serious.

"Can I have your name and address please, madam?" he asked briskly, and when these particulars and those of Mrs. Hibbert had been duly recorded, went on, "I'll get someone to call round this afternoon. Will you be in?"

"I'll wait in," Miss Frayne replied. "And who have I been speaking to?"

"Police Cadet Temple."

"Oh!" Then after a pause: "Are you sure you have put down everything I've told you?"

"Yes, don't worry, madam. There'll be somebody round."

"Shouldn't I have spoken to one of the detectives?"

"There's no one in the C.I.D. at the moment. They're all out."

"What about the duty sergeant or whatever he's called?"

"He's at lunch."

"Do you mean you're in charge of the whole station?" Miss Frayne asked in a scandalised voice.

"Just about. But not to worry, some of them are not very far away in the Canteen."

"I'm glad to hear that."

Nosey old bitch, Police Cadet Temple muttered to himself. Aloud he said, "Is that all, madam?"

"I suppose so."

"O.K. Then you just hang on and not worry and we'll have someone there quite soon."

And considerably to Miss Frayne's surprise, this is exactly what happened. A few minutes after two o'clock a black police car pulled up outside her house and a second or two later, there was a firm knock on the front door.

The officer who confronted her looked youthful enough to have been a cadet himself. He had a fresh, round face and the build of a middle-weight boxer.

"Miss Frayne? I'm P.C. Anker. I believe you telephoned the station a short time ago."

"Yes, about my neighbour Mrs. Hibbert. I'm sure something's happened to her."

By the time Miss Frayne had finished her recital, they had been joined by the driver of the car who introduced himself as P.C. Luff.

"Better go and have a look round the place, I suppose, Tom," P.C. Anker said, to his companion.

Miss Frayne watched them walk up Mrs. Hibbert's front path and try the door, then move round the outside of the house peering methodically in at all the windows.

"Kitchen window looks the best bet," P.C. Anker observed, when their tour of inspection was complete.

"Always is," his companion replied.

A minute later, Miss Frayne, who was watching intently from her own kitchen window, heard a sharp sound of splintering wood and saw P.C. Anker disappear into the house. Then the side-door was opened and P.C. Luff also disappeared inside.

In less than three minutes he re-appeared and dashed out to the waiting car. Before he had time to get in, however, Miss Frayne had also hurried out.

"Was I right? Is something the matter?" she enquired anxiously.

For a second or two he just stared at her in silence. Then almost curtly, he said, "Yes, something's the matter all right. The lady's dead. Looks as if she's been strangled."

9

2

DETECTIVE Chief Inspector Chudd was absorbed in mending a set of points in his sons' elaborately constructed model railway complex when the call came through informing him of Mrs. Hibbert's death. He sighed as he came downstairs from putting on a tie and a jacket. His wife was waiting in the hall and they exchanged a helpless look.

"Don't know when I shall get back, but I'll give you a call." He paused, knowing what was in her mind. "If I can still possibly make David's match, I will. But . . . well . . . ." He shrugged, aware that words were unnecessary and would only rub in the virtual certainty of his non-appearance at his son's first turnout for the school cricket eleven.

"He'll be terribly disappointed if you're not there, Peter. You know how he's been – "

"I know. Of course I'll be there if I can. But I'm sure he'll understand if I fail to make it."

Each of them, however, knew this was less than a pious hope, for David, aged thirteen and their eldest son, had been passing through a difficult patch which hadn't been helped by a change of school when his father had left the Yard on promotion and transfer to an outlying division. This had not only meant moving house but a change of school for all three of their sons. With Andrew aged eleven and Timmy aged nine, there'd been no difficulty, but David had not taken kindly to the disruption and would still have preferred the seventy-five minute journey each way to his old school than to have to adjust himself to a new one. But he had been overruled by his parents who had felt that the travelling would be too much for him each day and that he would settle down more easily than he imagined. But he hadn't; though his selection to play for the school cricket side had been the first indication of a break-through toward his acclimatisation, and his father had given a solemn promise to be present. The trouble was that a thirteen-year-old was unlikely to understand why police officers are not subject to the same rules of work and leisure as other people. And this would certainly be so in the case of a thirteen-year-old in David's present frame of mind.

"Well, try anyway," Kate Chudd said, knowing that there was nothing either of them could do about it. Unfortunately, the convenience of police officers wasn't consulted either by the perpetrators or the victims of crime. If it were, they might be able to work the five-day week that most people enjoyed. As it was, this was only the second day off Peter Chudd had had since being posted to the division a month ago.

He gave his wife a small wave before getting into the car which had arrived to pick him up. Thank God for Kate, anyway! he thought as they drove off. The move hadn't been easy for her either, but she had taken it in her stride and shown that police officers' wives need to be every bit as dedicated as their husbands. But David was certainly being a headache at the moment, which wouldn't have been so bad if his father wasn't also faced with problems of adjustment.

Peter Chudd was still just the right side of forty and had been in the Metropolitan Police for eighteen years. His climb up the ladder of promotion, though not meteoric, had been satisfactorily brisk and his recent appointment to Chief Inspector had been over the heads of several senior colleagues, amongst them the D.I. of the Division to which he had been posted.

D.I. Bracker belonged to the old sweat brigade and was a popular figure in the division, enjoying the sort of tolerant acceptance and respect that anything which has been around long enough is apt to acquire. At all events, it had been quite clear to Chudd soon after his arrival that his new colleagues had been hoping for their own man's promotion and his reception had to that extent been cool. A coolness increased, perhaps, by the suspicion with which someone from the Yard is greeted on returning to the field. And like his eldest son, Detective Chief

11

Inspector Chudd never found it easy to adjust himself to a new environment. He was sensitive to atmosphere and had a reserve which a police officer is better without.

His arrival in the division had been further complicated by the absence of Manton, the Detective Superintendent, who was on a special enquiry involving officers in a division the other side of London and who was likely to be away for at least a couple more weeks. So he had found himself almost at once in charge of the divisional C.I.D. and with not only a new job to learn but another to do at the same time.

As they turned into Mrs. Hibbert's road, he recognised the familiar scene. About two dozen people gathered in loose knots staring at the house as though they expected to see fireworks come out of the chimney and doing their best to ignore the efforts of two young constables to keep them moving.

Detective Inspector Bracker met him at the front door. "Everything's under control," he said, in an officious tone. "Photographer and fingerprint people are on their way. An ambulance came but I sent it packing. She's as dead as a sack of old potatoes and there's no point in disturbing her before Dr. Tracy's been." It seemed to Chudd as he listened that he was being assigned an under-instruction role. D.I. Bracker appeared to think that he had merely come along to see how a murder enquiry was initiated. "Incidentally," Bracker went on, "I've fixed that with the coroner. That Dr. Tracy should do the P.M. He's always our first choice here. If you step upstairs, I'll show you the body."

Just inside the front door was a small table, on which lay a sealed airmail letter, having apparently been placed there for posting. It was addressed to Mrs. Jessie Mellor, 14962 Hudson Avenue, Toronto, Canada. Picking it up by its edge, Chudd saw that the sender's name on the reverse side was Mrs. Florence Hibbert. With a thoughtful expression, he replaced it while Bracker stood impatiently at the foot of the stairs. Saturday's *Daily Express* lay beside the letter.

"Interesting to know what's in that letter," Chudd said as he followed the D.I. up to the bedroom.

"Don't imagine it'll help us find who killed the old girl. Not that I have much doubt about that myself."

"Meaning?"

"It's a clear case of murder committed in the course or furtherance of theft, as the Homicide Act puts it."

"That's a long way from knowing who did it."

"These cases always break sooner than you might think," Bracker replied with knowing superiority. "I'll have a check made of any Borstal boys on the run, as well as of the known thieves on our manor, and the odds are we'll turn up something. With luck we might even find a fingerprint or two."

Chudd said nothing, and passed into the bedroom. At first glance, the scene appeared perfectly normal. Then D.I. Bracker pulled up the counterpane which covered the bed and reached to the floor on either side, and said: "She's underneath."

Chudd knelt down and peered at the lumpy shape which Mrs. Hibbert had assumed in death. Her face was turned away from him, but he could see the ends of the floral scarf which had been wound tightly around her neck trailing out behind like two ribbons.

"Once the photographer has been, we'll dismantle the bed around her," Bracker said, smothering a yawn.

Chudd studied the floor, then walked out on to the landing.

"No sign of any scrape marks on the stair carpet or up here," he said. "Which seems to indicate that her murderer carried rather than dragged her."

"What's to say he didn't kill her right here in the bedroom?" Bracker asked.

"He may have done but there's no sign of that either. He certainly didn't kill her on the bed. Unless he stopped to remake it afterwards, which would seem unlikely."

D.I. Bracker shrugged to indicate that he regarded such speculation as pointless.

Chudd decided, while waiting for the pathologist and photographer to arrive, to examine the rest of the house.

"O.K., I'll go and organise things outside." Bracker said.

13

"What things?"

"Get those gawping bystanders dispersed for a start."

"More important, you might organize some house-to-house visiting. I want to know when Mrs. Hibbert was last seen alive and whether any of her neighbours can throw any light at all on what's happened."

"I was going to arrange that, anyway," Bracker said in a tone of faint huff.

"I'll want to interview anyone with any information, personally. And, Inspector," he called after Bracker's retiring back, "don't let either of us forget who's in charge of this enquiry."

He walked across the small landing and put his head round the door of another bedroom. It was smaller than Mrs. Hibbert's and the bed was unmade with the blankets folded on top of the mattress. There was a third bedroom but neither this nor the bathroom appeared to merit more than a cursory glance.

Pausing at the top of the stairs, he frowned as he tried to recollect the slightly curious feature that had half-caught his attention as he'd looked around. Yes, that was it! All those clocks! There were ticking clocks in every room, including the bathroom. And on the landing a baby grandfather stood sentinel, with another in the hall below. He went downstairs and began counting them. There were twelve in all. What a performance winding that lot up each week!

Reaching into his pocket, he felt for his pipe, but didn't find it. He returned upstairs and was gazing abstractedly round Mrs. Hibbert's bedroom, when one of the young D.C.'s looked in. "Lost something, sir?"

"My pipe. But don't worry. I must have put it down somewhere."

"You had it when you arrived, sir. I noticed."

"It'll turn up."

If I'm not careful, this'll become a pipe-hunt rather than a murder hunt, Chudd reflected with irritation. The trouble was he was still unused to the thing and was constantly mislaying it.

But Kate had persuaded him to give up cigarettes during the big cancer scare.

Fortunately, Dr. Tracy and the photographer chose this moment to arrive and Chudd was able to escape further speculation about where the infernal thing might be.

While they waited for the photographer to complete the first part of his job, Dr. Tracy peered about the bedroom like an estate agent on the track of dry rot while his secretary, a middle-aged female with a harassed expression, struggled to remove a hair from the tip of her ball-point pen.

"Liking it out on division?" Dr. Tracy asked, coming to rest at Chudd's side.

"It's not my first time, you know," Chudd replied in a faintly nettled tone. He was tired of being treated as though he had only recently stepped out of a space capsule.

"Bit different from the Yard, eh?"

"Indeed."

"Good thing to have a change. Stops the arteries getting furred up."

In Peter Chudd's experience, police officers might collect ulcers and nervous breakdowns and possibly burst a blood vessel or two. But furring up of their arteries seemed about the least likely hazard in the light of their physical activity.

"Finished?" Dr. Tracy asked the photographer. "Right! Then let's have that bed moved and I can see what I'm doing."

With the bed lifted away, Dr. Tracy knelt down beside the corpse and began a more detailed examination, while Chudd quietly watched him.

The photographer, who had taken a further two photographs showing Mrs. Hibbert exposed to full view, now retired to the other side of the room. He was a slim young man in blue blazer and flannels whom one wouldn't normally associate with the photography of victims of sudden death, which as it happened formed the major part of his daily round. But for several years now, the Metropolitan Police had employed civilian photographers such as he, in place of police officers trained in the art. He turned to Chudd.

"If you tell me what else you want me to take in the house, Chief Inspector, I'll get on with it. Then I'll see you later at the mortuary." He nodded at Dr. Tracy. "Know when he's going to do his P.M.?"

"Straightaway, I hope. Once he's finished here, we can shift the body and he can carry right on."

"O.K., then I won't wander far."

The photographer went out and Chudd turned his attention back to Dr. Tracy. "Any idea how long she's been dead?"

"As a preliminary view – and I stress the word *preliminary* – I'd say between two and three days. Does that fit in?"

"At the moment, there's nothing for it to fit in with. We haven't yet established when she was last seen alive."

Dr. Tracy rose from his knees. "All I can tell you now is that she was apparently strangled with that scarf round her neck and that her clothing appears to be intact. By which I mean no sexual interference."

An hour and a half later these findings were duly confirmed, with the additional information that she had most probably died on the Friday night or early Saturday morning.

Mrs. Hibbert now lay in one of the mortuary's refrigerated drawers. Each article of her clothing had been carefully sealed in a polythene bag and her various body samples were laid out in a neat row of jars and test tubes, to await transfer to the Metropolitan Police Laboratory by Detective-Sergeant Lancaster, whom Chudd had put in charge of all exhibits.

"Cause of death: asphyxia following compression of the neck by a ligature," Dr. Tracy intoned to his secretary. "Anything else you want to know before I go, Mr. Chudd?"

"I don't think so, sir."

"Where are we due next, Miss Plant?" he asked, turning again to his secretary.

"St. Pancras mortuary and then Southwark mortuary. And they did hope you'd have time to do a drowned man they pulled out of the river this morning."

"Then we must be on our corpse-strewn way immediately, Miss Plant," he said with a leer.

"What a way to earn a living!" Sergeant Lancaster observed, absent-mindedly fingering the jar containing Mrs. Hibbert's stomach contents.

Before leaving the mortuary, Chudd made a call to his wife to say that he didn't know what time he'd be home and that there was no hope of getting to David's match.

"Perhaps if he knows I'm on a murder enquiry, he'll be more understanding," he said.

"Because he'll be able to boast about it to the other boys, you mean?"

"Something like that."

"I suppose it is a subject for boasting?" Kate said doubtfully.

"I think it would have been when I was thirteen. Not that I'm suggesting he should or that I want him to. Anyway, I must go now, sweet. See you later."

"Try and be back before he goes to bed."

"I'll do my best."

He was met on his return to Mrs. Hibbert's house by the fingerprint officer.

"Is this yours, sir?" he enquired, holding out a pipe.

"Yes; thanks. Where was it?"

"On the hall table beneath the *Daily Express*. Thought it might be a vital clue, until someone mentioned it was probably yours. After all, didn't seem likely it was the deceased's. Though I know a few women do smoke pipes these days."

Chudd stuffed it in his pocket. About the only safe place to keep it if he wasn't going to have it forever being discovered in unlikely corners by his subordinates.

"Inspector Bracker been back since I left?"

"He was in and out about a quarter of an hour ago. I have an idea he's next door interviewing the old lady who reported the matter."

"You'll find me there, too, if I'm wanted."

Miss Frayne was sitting on an upright chair when Chudd knocked on the living-room door and walked in. The front-door had been wide open with a uniformed constable standing in the porch. Opposite her, more comfortably situated, were Nero and Detective-Inspector Bracker.

"You got my message?" Bracker enquired, after he had made the introductions.

"What message?"

"That I was here. I told young Carr to tell you."

"I didn't see Carr. However, perhaps you'd give me a résumé of what this lady has told you." When Bracker had finished speaking, Chudd said, "So you were away from home, Miss Frayne, from Friday evening until Sunday evening?"

"Yes, I'm afraid I was," Miss Frayne replied as though she herself had been caught out in some heinous crime.

"When did you last see Mrs. Hibbert?"

"On Friday afternoon. About four o'clock. I saw her put something in the dustbin. I think it was probably tea leaves," Miss Frayne explained, apparently in the belief that it was details such as this which solved murders.

"And what's all this about her lodger leaving?"

"That was on Friday, too."

"Miss Dunkley, did you say her name was?"

"Peggy Dunkley. She's games mistress at the Ellis Road Secondary Modern Girls' School."

"And when exactly on Friday did Miss Dunkley leave?"

"She went off as usual around half-past eight in the morning and she came back at half-past four to collect her things."

"Did you see her?"

"Oh, yes. I spoke to her. I went out to say good-bye when I saw her putting the suitcases into her little car."

"What time was that?"

"About five o'clock."

"After you had seen Mrs. Hibbert for the last time?"

"Yes."

"Did you know in advance that Miss Dunkley was leaving?"

"Yes, she'd told me on the Tuesday. She was very upset about it. Well, more than upset really. Cross. After all she'd been lodging at Mrs. Hibbert's for over two years now and she found it a very convenient arrangement."

"I gather then that Mrs. Hibbert asked her to go? It wasn't Miss Dunkley leaving of her own accord?"

"Oh, far from it. Mrs. Hibbert just told her that she wanted the bedroom by the weekend and would Miss Dunkley clear out by Friday at the latest."

"Sounds very sudden."

"It most certainly was. Peggy – that is Miss Dunkley – was most put out."

"Did Mrs. Hibbert give her any reason?"

"She told her that she had a cousin coming over from Canada for the summer and needed the room for her."

Chudd's mind went to the unposted airmail letter on the hall table.

"Do you happen to know the cousin's name, Miss Frayne?"

"I'm afraid not."

There was a minute's silence during which Nero recurled himself into a fresh position. Then Chudd said, "Did you have any discussion with Mrs. Hibbert about Miss Dunkley's departure?"

Miss Frayne pursed her lips and shook her head. "Mrs. Hibbert always kept herself to herself. She wasn't, I'm afraid, a very neighbourly person. She certainly never discussed her affairs with other people."

"But she and Miss Dunkley always got on all right?" Chudd asked in a probing voice.

"They lived their own lives. I mean, Miss Dunkley had a room there and that was about the extent of their contact."

"But presumably they used sometimes to sit and talk together?"

"I don't think very often," Miss Frayne said doubtfully. "Mrs. Hibbert wasn't an easy person to get on with. She wasn't at all a sociable person."

"Why did she bother with a lodger then?"

"For the money, I imagine."

"Do you know whether she and Miss Dunkley ever quarrelled?"

Miss Frayne looked embarrassed. "Before she gave Peggy notice, do you mean?"

"Ever quarrelled at any time?" Chudd repeated, leaning forward with an expression of alertness.

"Well, they certainly had a row the Tuesday evening that Mrs. Hibbert told Peggy she wanted the room for her cousin."

"Did you hear that?"

"I couldn't help it. I was weeding in the garden and their voices were raised. They were in the kitchen at the time."

"Did you hear any threats being used?"

"Threats? Oh, no, nothing like that!"

"What did you hear?"

"I heard Peggy say something like . . . ." Miss Frayne blushed. "Well, she did sometimes use rather strong language. She said it was 'bloody unreasonable' asking her to go at such short notice."

"And what did Mrs. Hibbert reply?"

"I heard her say, she couldn't help that, she required the room."

"Anything else?"

"No, that was all."

"Hmm." Chudd was thoughtful for a few seconds. "And did you ever hear them having rows on any other occasion?"

Miss Frayne looked uncomfortable. Had Chudd but known, she felt herself torn between loyalty to Peggy Dunkley and her civic sense of duty.

"I'm afraid I did," she replied at last, after sense of duty had triumphed. "About three or four times altogether."

"What did you actually hear?"

"Just raised voices."

"Do you know what they quarrelled about?"

Miss Frayne shook her hear. "Not specifically. Peggy used to say afterwards that Mrs. Hibbert had been particularly exasperating over something or other."

"What sort of things?" Chudd persisted.

"Mrs. Hibbert would accuse Peggy of leaving her sponge in the bathroom or of using the wrong saucepan to boil an egg. Little things like that."

"But apparently sufficient to spark off a row," Chudd

observed, rubbing the end of his nose, which was tickling. "Well, doubtless Miss Dunkley herself will be able to throw more light on their relationship." He turned to Inspector Bracker. "Anything further you think we ought to ask Miss Frayne before we depart?"

"Personally, I'd like to know why Miss Dunkley continued to live in a house with someone with whom she obviously didn't get on."

Miss Frayne smiled faintly. "Comfortable lodgings aren't all that easy to find and Peggy was very well suited there. I'm thankful to say that I've never had to live in lodgings, but I've always understood that there's no such thing as perfection. You take the best you can find and put up with the snags." She stood up. "If you've nothing else to ask me, mayn't I offer you a cup of tea? I'm sure you could do with one and the kettle is on. I've already given a cup to that young constable outside."

"I don't think either of us would say no to that kind offer," Chudd replied.

Bracker grimaced at her back as she went out of the room.

"Bloody cups of tea in the middle of murder enquiries," he muttered. Chudd noticed, however, that he not only noisily swallowed the tea when it arrived but accepted a second cup.

As they made to leave, Chudd said, "I'd like to thank you, Miss Frayne, for telephoning the police station. It was very public spirited of you. If everyone was as co-operative, our job would be that much simpler."

Miss Frayne glowed with pleasure at this accolade. "Well, I thought it was my duty to report it," she replied complacently.

"You were absolutely right. We shall almost certainly want to have another talk with you later on when we have unearthed a bit more." Chudd turned back in the doorway. "Incidentally, there is one further matter I ought to have asked you about, do you know who Mrs. Hibbert's next of kin is? I can find out, but it'll save time if you happen to know."

"I'm afraid I don't. I've never heard her mention any relative."

"Except the cousin in Canada?"

"I only heard of her through Peggy."

"Doubtless Miss Dunkley will be able to help us about that, too, then."

"She never had any visitors," Miss Frayne added. "I'd have noticed. As I've said, she kept herself very much to herself."

The young constable who had removed himself to the pavement gate grinned as the two C.I.D. men came out. Then looked sheepish as Miss Frayne called out from the front-door, "Would you like another cup of tea, officer?"

Under the compulsion of Inspector Bracker's glare, he shook his head. "No, thanks."

"What do you think of that old girl?" Bracker asked as they made their way back to Mrs. Hibbert's.

"She gave the impression of telling the truth."

"The old busybody."

"Who are we to complain?"

"It looks as though this Dunkley woman has got a bit of answering to do. Damned fishy her leaving the very day of the deceased's death and after a quarrel, too."

"She's certainly the next person to be seen," Chudd remarked. "In fact, I propose to go and find her now. I'll leave you to go through Mrs. Hibbert's things, and when you've finished, perhaps you'd see the place is locked and sealed."

"If that's what you want," Bracker said in a sour tone.

Chudd looked at his watch. It was tempting to drive via David's school and stop for ten minutes, but a second's reflection told him that this just wasn't practicable. Time was of the essence in these initial stages of the enquiry. It was one thing to drink a cup of Miss Frayne's tea, another to go and watch his son play cricket. He consoled himself with the thought that in any event he would most probably have found David's side batting and David himself out of sight in the pavilion.

It was around half-past five when his driver drew up outside Ellis Road Secondary Modern Girls' School, which reminded Chudd of a series of inter-connected glass cubes. On the whole he was in favour of much modern architecture, but it did seem to him that the modern classroom had become a shop window. However, it was Elwick Common's newest building and Chudd wished the police station could borrow some of its amenities.

The place appeared to be deserted and he had paced past acres of sheet glass before discovering anyone.

"Excuse me, can you tell me where I can find Miss Dunkley?" he asked through an open window.

The female inside who was sitting at a desk correcting exercise books looked up with a start.

"Haven't a clue. Dunkley? Dunkley? I'm afraid I'm new here this term, I don't know all the staff yet."

"She's the games mistress."

"Oh yes, I know who you mean. I have an idea it's her afternoon off."

"How can I find out where she lives?"

"There's an address book in the staff room. Actually, it's a staff register but it contains addresses as well. Do you want me to come with you?"

"I'd be grateful if you would."

Doubt suddenly clouded the woman's expression. "I suppose it's in order, but I've no idea who you are."

"I'm Detective Chief Inspector Chudd."

Her jaw sagged. "Oh! I didn't realise you were police."

Chudd was uncertain from her tone whether this fact had removed, or had merely served to increase, her doubts.

"I'm not going to arrest Miss Dunkley or anything like that, but she may be able to assist us in an enquiry."

"Good heavens, you really do say that. I thought it was only newspaper reporting."

"I'm afraid I don't follow you," Chudd said.

"That bit about assisting you in your enquiries. It always appears in the papers when you're grilling a suspect. I've always thought it a charming euphemism."

"Look, Miss . . ."

"Green."

"Look, Miss Green, I wonder if we could find that register. I don't have an awful lot of time."

"Yes, of course, I'm so sorry. If you go to that door on the right, I'll let you in and take you to the staff room."

As they walked along one of the covered passage ways which connected two of the cubes, Chudd said, "It would probably be as well if you didn't noise it around that I wanted to see Miss Dunkley. Sometimes people are a bit sensitive about it becoming known that they've been interviewed by the police."

"I would be myself. And of course in a place like this, rumours multiply faster than germs in a flu epidemic. No, I won't say anything. Anyway, I'm too new here to be other than circumspect. You don't start stirring up trouble until you cease to mind the consequences."

In the staff room, his guide fetched from a cupboard an indexed exercise book with a well-thumbed cover.

Peggy Dunkley's was the only name under "D"; the address "c/o Mrs. Hibbert, 14, Cresta Drive" had been neatly ruled through and beneath appeared in fresh ink, "c/o Miss Smith, 27, North Avenue."

Thanking Miss Green for her help, Chudd returned to his car, and fifteen minutes later, having picked up Detective-Sergeant Roberts at the station on the way, was knocking on Miss Smith's front door in a street as drear in appearance as the point of the compass from which it took its name. Moreover, Chudd could hardly feel that a sparse line of sickly lime trees justified the designation 'avenue'.

The woman who answered was a muscular-looking blonde somewhere in her mid-thirties. Her hair was drawn back behind the ears and she was dressed in ski-ing outfit, with tapered blue trousers and a sweater of the same colour which was covered with white fleur de lys. But perhaps her most striking feature was the determined set of her mouth and jaw.

"Miss Dunkley?"

"Yes." Her tone held a don't-give-me-any-nonsense note. Chudd introduced himself and his companion. "We'd like

24

to have a word with you, Miss Dunkley. May we come in?"

"I suppose so. Miss Smith's out, so we can probably use her front-room if it's not going to take long. Is it about one of the girls?"

Chudd shook his head. "No, it's about Mrs. Hibbert."

Peggy Dunkley's expression hardened and she said in a tone of distinct belligerence, "*What* about Mrs. Hibbert? She's not someone I particularly wish to be reminded of. If she's been making any accusations . . . ." She broke off. "Well, what about her?"

"She's dead."

"Dead! That certainly comes as a bit of a shock. When did she die?"

"Over the weekend," Chudd replied evasively.

"I take it you know I used to be her lodger?" She went on without waiting for an answer, "Of course you must know, that's why you're here. What is it you want with me?"

"When did you last see her alive?"

"Last Friday afternoon when I packed up and left."

"About what time was that?"

"Half-past four or thereabouts."

"And where?"

"Where! In the house."

"Yes, but where in the house?"

Peggy Dunkley appeared about to answer, then frowned. "As a matter of strict accuracy I didn't actually see her. Perhaps I'd better explain. She was in her bedroom—Mrs. Hibbert that is—the radio was on and I just called out good-bye to her as I carried my last suitcase downstairs."

"Did she reply?"

"No. But that wasn't very surprising as we weren't exactly parting on amicable terms. My 'good-bye' had not carried any note of affection, I may add."

"Weren't you surprised when you got no reply?" Sergeant Roberts asked.

"Not a bit. I imagined she had deliberately shut herself in her bedroom to avoid seeing me."

"You didn't think of knocking on her door?"

"I did not," Peggy Dunkley retorted vehemently, "and nor would you have done in my place."

"You can't definitely say that she was in the bedroom?"

"Yes I can, because the radio was on."

"That's not proof."

"Look, the only time Mrs. Hibbert had her bedroom radio on was when she was in there."

There was a pause before Chudd asked, "So when *did* you actually last see her?"

"I suppose it must have been the Thursday evening."

"You didn't see her on Friday morning?"

"No, she wasn't often up by the time I left. Anyway, we reached the sort of accommodation whereby we contrived to avoid each other in the mornings. I'm certainly not at my best then and she was inclined to be difficult at any hour of the day."

"How long had you lodged at her house?"

"Getting on for two and a half years."

"And why did you leave?" Chudd asked.

If he entertained any hopes of hearing something contradictory of the second-hand account passed on by Miss Frayne, they were to be quickly dashed.

"I didn't leave, I was thrown out," she said with a harsh laugh which was as far removed from amusement as a dog's bark from human speech. "I was given precisely four days to pack up and go."

"Why such short notice?"

"If I'd wanted to be difficult, I could have insisted on a week's notice, but in the circumstances I was so disgusted, I didn't even want to stand on my rights. And moreover she said she particularly wanted my room by the weekend."

"For what reason?"

"Some cousin coming over from Canada."

"Would that be Mrs. Mellor who lives in Toronto?"

Peggy Dunkley looked at the officers sharply. "I believe that is her name. I've never met her, but I once posted a letter for Mrs. Hibbert with that name on the envelope."

"You can probably help us, Miss Dunkley, over Mrs. Hibbert's next of kin. Do you know who it is?"

Peggy Dunkley stared abstractedly at the floor between her legs and shook her head. "I don't know of any family at all, apart from the cousin in Canada. From something she once said I gathered she had a younger sister who died some years ago. But she never mentioned any nephews or nieces and certainly she never received any visits from family while I was staying there, so far as I know."

"Do you know if she had a solicitor?"

Peggy Dunkley's mouth twisted into a smile. "As a matter of fact I do know as I happened to see a letter lying about once. I can't remember the address, except that it was somewhere in W.1., but the name of the firm was Dann, Hicks and Company."

"And it was clear from the letter that they were Mrs. Hibbert's solicitors?"

"Yes, it was," Peggy Dunkley said shortly. In a slightly gruff tone she added, "Don't run away with the idea that I used to go through her private correspondence when she wasn't around. This letter was sitting on the kitchen table. It simply said that the writer would look forward to seeing her on the arranged date. The whole letter wasn't more than a couple of lines."

"The main thing is you remember the name of the firm. That's a big help," Chudd replied in a tone which concealed his thoughts about those who read other people's letters. "And since you left Mrs. Hibbert's house around half-past four last Friday, have you been back at all?"

"Certainly not. Why do you ask that particular question?"

"Because I wanted to know the answer."

"Yes, but . . ." Her mind seemed suddenly to change direction. "Incidentally you haven't told me what Mrs. Hibbert died of. Did she have a heart attack?"

"She was murdered. Strangled."

"Good God! That at least explains all your questions! Who on earth strangled her?"

"We don't know—yet."

"Well, I can assure you that I didn't," she said emphatically.

"That suggestion has never been made."

"Not overtly, I know, but you can eliminate me from your list of suspects. Mrs. Hibbert and I may not have parted on very cordial terms, but I had no thought of murdering her."

"Someone did," Chudd said flatly. He was inclined to regard Peggy Dunkley's denials as unsolicited circulars being thrust through his letter-box. Fixing her intently with a hard gaze, he went on, "Do you recall noticing what was on the hall table when you left on Friday afternoon?"

"Nothing."

"No letters?"

"Definitely nothing. I left my key there and the surface was bare."

"Your key?"

"My key to Mrs. Hibbert's front-door. I was going to hand it to her personally, but since she never gave me the opportunity, I left it on the hall table where I knew she'd be bound to see it."

Chudd was thoughtful for a time. "What sort of key was it?"

"A Yale. Had a small piece of red ribbon tied to it."

"And you're certain you left it where you say?"

"Of course I'm certain."

A few minutes later, Chudd rose. "I think that's about all for the present, Miss Dunkley. You'll probably be required to attend the inquest and we shall be seeing you again, too."

"When will the inquest be?"

"The coroner's likely to open it tomorrow and then adjourn while our enquiries go ahead."

"It'll be very inconvenient if I'm wanted to-morrow."

"You won't be. Tomorrow's proceedings will be purely formal. The only witnesses will be the pathologist and myself."

"I suppose this is bound to be in all the papers?"

"For certain."

She tossed her head in a gesture of exasperation. "That means it'll be all over the school in no time. My connection with the matter, I mean. I shouldn't be surprised if I'm not tactfully asked to leave," she added bitterly.

"That would seem a bit harsh."

"You don't know some of our parents."

"Surely the headmistress will see them off."

"You don't know her either."

Chudd made a small Gallic gesture of resignation. "I hope it won't turn out as badly as you fear." When he and Sergeant Roberts were back in the car, he said, "What impression did you form of her?"

"She seemed to be telling the truth. She corroborated what Miss Frayne had told you."

"That could be because what Miss Frayne told us was what that woman had told her."

"Yes, I was overlooking that." He was pensive for a second or two. "I would certainly think she'd be capable of committing murder given the right circumstances."

Chudd smiled. "Surely that applies to each one of us. But I agree that Peggy Dunkley would appear to be of the right physical and mental stature for this particular crime. I wonder if she did leave the door key as she says. If it isn't found in the house, a whole new field of speculation will have opened up, because it'll either mean that she has lied to us or that the murderer removed it."

"I can't see why the murderer should take it."

"Nor can I. In which case, it would have been possible for Miss Dunkley to have returned to the house on Friday night and let herself in . . ."

"I tell you another thing which is puzzling me, sir, and that is how Saturday's *Daily Express* came to be on the hall table if, as the medical evidence suggests, Mrs. Hibbert was strangled either on Friday night or in the early hours of Saturday morning."

Chudd nodded. "I know. It doesn't seem to make sense. I suppose it's possible that Dr. Tracy has got his times wrong, but the difficulty will be in getting him to admit it. And if he hasn't, the only inference is that someone was in the house on

Saturday morning after the paper boy had made his round."

Detective-Inspector Bracker was at the station when they arrived back. He pointed to a cardboard carton on his desk. "I've put all her personal property which might be of any interest in there."

"Happen to notice a Yale key?" Chudd enquired.

"I think I saw one in her handbag," Bracker reached inside the carton, produced a woman's handbag and shook out the contents on to the desk. "Yes, here's a key," he said, holding up one on a cheap metal ring.

"You haven't seen one with a bit of red ribbon attached to it?"

Bracker pursed his lips. "No. This is the only key I've come across and I went through every drawer in the place. Incidentally, I've checked that Miss Frayne did spend the weekend away from home, but she was only about a couple of miles away and she was on her own apart from a couple of kids she was looking after."

"But there's nothing to suggest she murdered her next-door neighbour," Chudd remarked.

"As far as I'm concerned they're all suspects until we can eliminate them." Bracker replied bluntly. "And anyone who thinks otherwise is, in my view, dangerously mistaken."

Ignoring this truculently expressed observation, Chudd peered into the carton containing Mrs. Hibbert's belongings as if it might have been a bran-tub. Then dipping in his right hand he pulled out the unposted airmail letter.

"Going to steam it open?" Inspector Bracker enquired with interest.

"No, I'm going to slit it open," Chudd said quietly, and promptly proceeded to do so.

The other two officers watched him unfold the letter and saw a frown spread across his brow as he read it.

"Hmm. What do you make of this?" he said, without looking up. "It's dated last Friday, incidentally. 'Dear Jessie, I'm glad to hear that you will definitely be coming over in the autumn. It must be thirty years nearly since we met, but I still remember that Great Uncle Arthur was my grandfather's favourite brother. You'll see great changes in England, not many of them for the better. I shall be sixty-four next birthday, but keep pretty well on the whole. My lodger, whom I've had for two years, is leaving to-day. I think I've mentioned her in one of my earlier letters. She teaches games at a girls' school in the district. You'll be able to use her room when you come. Nero, my cat, caught two mice last week. Let me have more details of your visit nearer the time. Your affectionate cousin, Florence Hibbert'."

He looked up. "It's only May now and if Cousin Jessie isn't expected till the autumn, what was the urgency to get rid of the Dunkley female? And why did the deceased pretend her cousin was arriving this last weekend?"

"We only have Dunkley's word that that was the reason for her being asked to leave."

"Precisely. Either she's deliberately deceived us or the deceased deliberately deceived her. Now, I wonder which!"

3

It was twenty minutes to midnight when Chudd arrived home. Since he had always been relatively unaware of his physical surroundings – or rather he was aware of them, but never let them possess his mind – he had, more quickly than Kate, come to accept their semi-detached as home. It provided a sound roof over their heads, had a small garden and looked precisely the same as a hundred other houses in that and adjoining streets. It belonged to the thirties when Elwick Common had burgeoned into a white collar dormitory suburb and town planning meant no more than houses in straight rows. The house was in darkness, but on the table in the kitchen he found a flask of tea, some freshly cut cheese sandwiches and a note from his wife. It read :

"David is determined to stay awake until you get back.

Can't promise the same for myself."

It was timed 10.50.

Armed with one of the sandwiches and a mug of tea, Chudd crept upstairs and paused outside his son's bedroom door which was ajar. One palliative which they had been able to offer David when they'd moved was a room to himself. In their previous house the three boys had shared an enormous bedroom, but now Andrew and Timmy were on their own. Stealthily he eased the door open and side-stepped inside. As he did so, he heard the rustle of bedclothes and the light was switched on. Like most schoolboys, David had erected a Heath Robinson-like system to enable him to operate the light switch by the door from his bed. The main element consisted of yards of string which festooned the room as if it had been woven by an inebriated spider.

"Did I wake you up?"

"I wasn't properly asleep."

Chudd sat down on the edge of bed. "Mind if I have my supper here?"

David propped himself up on his elbows and shook his head. His hair was tousled and his nose shiny. He had his father's broad head and cool, watchful eyes. But cool eyes didn't necessarily denote a placid temperament or an easy equilibrium along the path of growing-up.

"How did the match go?"

"We lost."

"Badly?"

"By two wickets."

"How many runs did you make?"

"Eighteen."

"Was that highest score?"

"No, a boy called Jackson made twenty-three."

"I call that a good start, David."

"Might have been worse, I suppose," he said in the self-deprecation which borders on complacence. "I made a catch as well."

"A good one?"

"In the slips."

"That's one place I could never field. Worse than playing in goal at soccer."

David grinned. "I like it. Keeps you on your toes all the time."

"Anyway, that's a pretty good start, David. They're sure to keep you in the side now, aren't they?"

"Mr. Alver, he's the master in charge of cricket, said I'd be in the next match."

"Splendid. When is it?"

"On Friday. Will you be able to come, Dad?"

"Depends how this case goes. I had every intention, as you know, of coming this afternoon, but then had to go off on this enquiry."

"Yes, Mum told me. Have you caught the chap yet?"

"'Fraid not. Don't even know who we're looking for."

David let out a cavernous yawn, which he made no attempt to stifle.

"It's time you were asleep."

"I'm not tired."

"No, but you will be tomorrow morning and I shall get the blame."

"Don't go yet, Dad. Honestly, I'm not sleepy."

Chudd glanced at his watch. "Three more minutes then, because even if you're not, I am. Apart from cricket, how are things going?"

"So, so!" David conceded, sticking out his lower lip in a gesture of uncertainty. "I'll never think it's as good a school as King John's."

Chudd knew better than to argue with his son. Any attempt at overt persuasion had all along been doomed to failure. Indeed, had merely exacerbated the situation.

"I wonder whether you'd have made the cricket eleven this

term if you'd stayed there." he observed in an apparently thoughtful way.

David chewed at the corner of his mouth. "I couldn't possibly have. They have seven old colours from last year still at the school and at least half the second eleven as well. I should think I might just have got into the second eleven."

Chudd nodded thoughtfully, then swallowing the remains of his tea, he got up. "'Night, old lad," he said, giving his son's shoulder an affectionate pat. "Shall I turn your light out or is the system operating both ways to-night?"

For answer, David began tugging at the end of string which was fastened to the head of his bed. An ornament toppled from a shelf and a small bookcase made a forward lurch, but with a strained click the light went off.

"See! Good-night, Dad."

The first thing Chudd did on reaching his office the next morning was to switch on the two lights without whose aid one could scarcely see across the room, even on a midsummer's day. The police station had been built when Elwick Common was a village surrounded by green fields, long before it became part of the greater London conurbation. It was a double-fronted building of blackened brick and its interior consisted of dingy corridors, two dark and precipitous stair-cases and rooms the size of broom cupboards. Chudd felt that the man who had designed it had shown a perverse genius for wasting space. And as usual the C.I.D. had come off worst. He sat down and began to read through the small pile of statements relating to Mrs. Hibbert's death which had been placed on his desk. For the most part they came from people who lived in the same street and who had been questioned about the last time they saw her alive. They were generally vague and/or unhelpful in tenor. But at least there was no one who purported to have seen her alive on the Saturday and Chudd regarded this as a gain. Although there was the mystery of Saturday's newspaper folded on the hall table to be explained, he felt that the medical evidence as to time of death must be the sheet anchor of his enquiry, and consequently anything which didn't fit in with this had to be subjected to a process of rationalisation. If any of the neighbours had reported seeing her alive on the Saturday, he would have felt bound to impeach their recollection.

One of the statements was that of Kenny Wright, aged thirteen, who declared that he had been delivering Mrs. Hibbert's daily newspaper for the past eighteen months and that on the Saturday morning in question he had stuck it through the front-door letter-box at about half-past seven, his usual time. He went on to say that he never did see Mrs. Hibbert on his rounds and that he always left the paper sticking through the slit and did not push it right through so that it fell on the floor. He concluded by saying that he hadn't noticed anything different on Saturday morning from any other.

With the statements was a message informing Chudd that Mr. Dann of Dann, Hicks and Company was Mrs. Hibbert's solicitor and was expected in his office around ten o'clock. Chudd looked at his watch and saw that it was a few minutes after nine.

He turned to the report of overnight crime. There'd been two burglaries, one alleged rape by a man on his ex-wife, and a fight outside a public house at closing time in which a youth had been knifed but had sustained nothing worse than an inch and a half cut on his right forearm.

Could be worse, he reflected, though heaven knew how he could spare anyone to go and investigate those matters as they merited. Shortage of officers and an increase in crime always seemed to him to be in direct ratio, and though he accepted and welcomed all the new scientific developments in the solution of crime, he still regarded the man on the beat as the best preventive. Unhappily, the man on the beat was becoming as extinct as certain species of the African jungle.

His meditations were interrupted by the door being thrown open and Detective Inspector Bracker entering, hat on head and raincoat over his arm.

"I'm at the Court of Criminal Appeal to-day. Don't expect

to be back before this afternoon. It's the Sefton appeal."
Observing Chudd's expression he went on, "But of course
that was all before you got here. Two brothers called Sefton
and a man named Archer got seven years apiece for assault
and robbery at a sub post-office."

Chudd nodded. "What are the grounds of appeal?"

"God knows! They're three of the ripest villains I've come
across. They should have been sent down for at least ten.
Trouble was they came before one of those temporary judges
at the Bailey and he leant over so far backwards to be fair to
the defence he almost fell off his bloody great chair."

With this scathing condemnation of the judiciary, Bracker
departed, and Chudd returned his attention to the papers on
his desk. He wondered how long Bracker would maintain
this front of insolent aggression and equally how long he would
endure it without a major showdown. What held him back
was the degree of compassion he felt for the inspector's
situation. His reaction to the humiliation at being passed over
for promotion manifested itself in an attitude of patronising
truculence and, galling though this was, Chudd decided to
put up with it as long as he could. To ride out the storm of
the other's abraded vanity.

He groaned aloud as he found two more No. 1 dockets
at the bottom of the pile. These had now become as familiar
as motor-scooters, young men with beards and girls in sloppy
sweaters and jeans. In short, they were a current feature of
life—a detestable feature in the life of a Detective Chief
Inspector. No. 1 dockets was the name given to complaints
made against the police by members of the public, and the
instruction was they had to receive priority treatment. This
in itself was an indication of the melancholy state of disrepair
into which the public and the police had allowed their mutual
respect to fall. The public was mistrustful, the police resentful.
A handful of miserable cases had necessarily tarnished their
image, but now the public seemed intent on a campaign of
smear. Or so it sometimes appeared to Chudd as he spent
hours investigating what were usually baseless and often

malicious complaints against decent, hard-working colleagues. Surely they didn't deserve the odium of so much bad publicity. And the result of all this? That half the nation's police force spent its time investigating allegations against the other half, and that Chudd now found himself staring with glassy-eyed despair at two of these allegations in particular.

The first was a complaint by a Borstal boy that the flick-knife of which he had been convicted of being in possession had been planted on him by the arresting officer who had, moreover, assaulted him in the detention room at the station, stolen a pound note from his wallet and committed perjury at the trial. For better measure he added that he had also been framed on a previous occasion when he had been convicted of a similar offence. The present complaint reached Chudd's desk via the boy's father, his M.P., the Home Secretary and the Commissioner. It bore all the indications of urgency and requiring immediate action. Chudd closed the docket and stuck it underneath the other papers.

The second one contained an allegation by a man, known to all the officers stationed at Elwick Common for his virulent anti-police attitude, that Police Constable Farquharson had deliberately tried to set fire to the complainant's car by throwing a cigarette end down near its petrol tank. This diabolical attempt having failed, the officer had kicked one of the wheels as he passed, thereby causing "malicious damage". The letter concluded with a demand for protection from further police persecution or the writer would feel obliged to give his views to the Press.

Chudd reflected grimly that those two matters could together occupy a whole week of his time, in order that the public might be satisfied it was receiving its pound of flesh. Somehow, a sense of values seemed to have become the distorted element in national life.

Shoving this docket beneath the other, he tried t forget his own sense of grievance at what he could only regard as an intolerable abuse of police procedure and put through a call to Mr. Dann.

The solicitor hadn't yet arrived in his office, but his secretary assured Chudd that he would be able to see him if he came any time during the morning. Accordingly, after a short conference to co-ordinate the day's enquiries, he set off to see Mr. Dann, whose firm was located near Baker Street.

Fifty minutes later Chudd was seated in the solicitor's sanctum. Mr. Dann turned out to be a man of about sixty with a weathered face and an untidy thatch of undistinguished grey hair. His office was almost Dickensian in its discomfort, and the chair on which Chudd was sitting felt like a sackload of distended springs.

"As you will appreciate, Chief Inspector, this news came as a great shock to me," Mr. Dann said in the weighted tones which lawyers are wont to acquire. "We become used, if sadly so, to the deaths of our clients from time to time, but to have one die violently in this fashion is something quite shocking. Yes, quite shocking. We had acted for Mrs. Hibbert even since her husband's death and for him before, so you can tell what a terrible shock this has been." He shook his head as if to emphasize his feeling. "It's hard to conceive of anything less agreeable than to have a client murdered."

"Except to have a client commit one," Chudd was tempted to add. Instead he said, "Can you tell me who Mrs. Hibbert's next of kin is?"

"She has no near relatives, you know. Indeed, her nearest is a cousin in Canada."

"Would that be Mrs. Mellor?"

"Ah, you know the lady's name. Yes, that is she."

"Are you aware of any plans Mrs. Mellor has for visiting this country in the near future?"

Mr. Dann assumed an expression of surprise. "No, no. Should I have?"

Chudd decided to tell him of the letter and also of Peggy Dunkley's abrupt departure from his client's house.

"No, I knew nothing of that at all," he said in a puzzled tone, "but I'm sure there must be some perfectly simple explanation."

"If you can think of one, I'd be delighted to hear it."

"Oh, there must be! There must be!"

"May I ask when you were last in touch with Mrs. Hibbert?"

"Quite recently." The corners of Mr. Dann's mouth went down as if the recollection was a matter for disapproval. "As a matter of fact, Chief Inspector, she was due to come and see me tomorrow." Chudd waited, and the solicitor after an apparent inner struggle added, "About her will."

"About her will!" Chudd's tone held a note of hopeful interest.

"I obviously can't discuss the contents of my client's last will and testament . . . ."

"But surely that's just what you can do," Chudd broke in. "Now that she's dead, the will's going to be proved and it'll be public property soon, anyway."

Mr. Dann frowned. He didn't like being told his business quite so bluntly, particularly by a police officer, and even if he had rather perched himself out on a limb.

"There's no need to remind you, I'm sure, of the absolute privilege of all communications passing between a solicitor and his client. However, I think I can properly tell you that Mrs. Hibbert was apparently contemplating a change in her will."

"May I start by knowing who is the main beneficiary under her existing will?"

"Mrs. Mellor."

"And what was the proposed change?" Chudd asked, ignoring Mr. Dann's expression of pained reproof.

"I can't tell you. By which I mean, I don't know." He laced his hands on top of the desk and went on in the tone he might have used for reasoning with a headstrong child. "Let me try and explain. About twelve days ago, Mrs. Hibbert wrote a letter saying she wished to come and see me and suggesting three o'clock tomorrow afternoon. I replied by letter confirming that that would be quite convenient. Then a few days later—it would have been last Tuesday or Wednesday—she 'phoned to ask if it would be all right if she came in the morning instead and I took the opportunity of asking her the reasons for the appointment." Mr. Dann paused and flicked a speck of dust off his shiny black sleeve. "I pointed out that it sometimes made interviews easier if one knew their subject in advance."

"And it was then that she mentioned changing her will?"

Mr. Dann waved a hand as if to ward off the attentions of a mosquito.

"Hear me out, Chief Inspector, hear me out. She said nothing at all about *changing* her will. That was merely the impression I gained. All Mrs. Hibbert said was that her visit to me *concerned* her will."

"Surely that could only have meant she wished to change it?"

"That was certainly my strong impression, but let us be clear, it wasn't what she actually said."

Chudd thought for a moment. "Well, may I ask you this, was there anything about her will which required consultation?"

"Nothing."

"When did she make it, by the way?"

"About five or six years ago."

"And before that?"

"Her whole estate was bequeathed to a certain charity." Mr. Dann grimaced. "One devoted to the welfare of cats, if you must know."

"So she suddenly cut cats out of her will and substituted this cousin in Canada?"

"Crudely expressed, but accurate."

"And you have no idea what she had in mind?"

"I fear not, only the supposition that she was proposing to make a fresh will."

"A completely fresh one?"

"That was my impression."

"What a pity you didn't ask her for details when you were talking to her on the 'phone," Chudd said, more thinking aloud than otherwise.

Mr. Dann frowned, and in a chilly tone said, "One's clients do not care to discuss the private nature of their wills over the telephone and naturally one doesn't press them to do so, except in a situation of great urgency. And there was no indication that this was particularly urgent."

"No, I quite follow. After all, you were hardly to know that your client was about to fall victim to murder."

"Thank you for that consolation."

After some further discussion concerning the winding-up of Mrs. Hibbert's estate, Mr. Dann asked, "Can I now go ahead and arrange the funeral?"

"It's for the coroner to release the body."

The solicitor wrinkled his nose in distaste. "May I take it there'll be no difficulty about that?"

"It may be a little early . . . ."

"How long do these matters usually take?"

"One can't tell. Sometimes, quite a long while."

"And what about my client all this time?"

"In cold storage."

"Really, Chief Inspector, you do rather manage to reduce the solemnity of the occasion to the level of the butcher's shop."

"Surely, it's her soul that matters, or so we're taught."

"Her soul has reached its haven wherever that may be," Mr. Dann said a trifle testily. "And in any event it wasn't in my care. I'm concerned only with her earthly remains." He paused, then said with considerable vehemence. "Anyway, dammit man, you can't leave bodies about unburied! It's unchristian, unhygienic and extremely distressing to the relatives."

"Mrs. Hibbert hasn't got any to become distressed. Incidentally, will you be cabling Mrs. Mellor in Canada?"

"Immediately. It's my duty as Mrs. Hibbert's executor."

"If she comes over, I shall want to see her," Chudd said, and made a mental note to make his own enquiries about Mrs. Mellor, whether she came or not. "I haven't asked you this, Mr. Dann, but how much has Mrs. Hibbert left?"

"Between thirty and forty thousand pounds."

Chudd sighed. Not a wild fortune, by the standards of some, but a very agreeable legacy, especially if it were unexpected. He wondered if Mrs. Mellor had known what was coming to her. For a second or two his mind drifted off into a fantasy in which some unheard-of relative in another continent left him an equal sum.

Bidding Mr. Dann good-bye, he went out into the street to find no sign of his car. A minute later, however, it came into sight round a corner.

"Sorry about that, sir," the driver said, "but I got a bloody parking ticket. Just left it for five minutes to go and have a cup of tea and when I got back, there was this ticket."

Chudd sounded resigned when he spoke. "What have you done about it?"

"I found the yellow-banded dolt who put it there and told him to stuff it in his knapsack. I said if he didn't he'd be reported for impeding a senior officer in the course of a murder enquiry."

"Oh, my God, I should think that's put us on the muck heap! These traffic wardens don't take kindly to that sort of thing. Furthermore, once the ticket's made out, probably nothing less than an Act of Parliament can rescind it."

"This one'll be rescinded all right," the driver said grimly.

"Well, if it's not, don't come to me for a sub toward the fine."

In a clearly black frame of mind the driver vented his feelings on the car by crashing a gear. Meanwhile, Chudd turned his own thoughts to the next stage of the investigation. Although there were still several leads to be followed, nothing in the way of a definite clue had so far emerged. Nothing which would enable him to issue the description of someone who, it was believed, might be able to assist the police in their enquiries. And until there was such a clue, it was like groping around in a dark room. Frustrating and, finally, unnerving.

On arrival back at the station in Elwick Common, Chudd went to his dingy office on the first floor. It contained but two chairs and its desk was scarcely visible beneath all the paper which now swamped a modern police force. The walls were hidden by graphs and charts reflecting the division's contribution toward the general crime boom.

This small, now empty, room had been dignified by the Press with the designation "murder headquarters". It wasn't sufficient for their readers to know that the station was the base for enquiries, a room had to be identified in the same way as the buttons in Moscow and Washington which wait to play their tiny but vital part in the destruction of civilisation. This was the age of audience participation.

The first impact of Press interest in the case would soon be over, however, and the police would be left to get on with their slogging routine until something brought the pack back again. Last night, the later editions of both evening papers had given it the full treatment. "Widow Found Strangled," cried one: "Murder Victim Under Bed" yelled the other. But already, one day later, the item had been relegated to a few lines under the respectable heading of "Home News". A murder without any overtones of sex can't hope to sustain public interest for longer than its initial discovery. Chudd wondered whether the broadcast appeal for information from anyone who might have seen or heard anything in connection with Mrs. Hibbert's death would bring forth more than silence or, worse, the effusions of the mentally unstable. The announcer's tone, drier than tonic water, would make it sound as undramatic as the fat-stock prices.

He had just decided to go and have a further word with Peggy Dunkley when Detective Sergeant Roberts came into the room.

"Hello, sir, you just back?" Chudd nodded. "Learn anything of interest from the old lady's solicitor?"

Chudd told him about the will situation, which Roberts clearly thought worthy only of dismissal.

"Sherlock Holmes's cases may have revolved round changed wills and forged wills, but it just doesn't happen these days, if it ever did in those."

"I agree it's a bit corny, but it's something we must explore until we've finally established a motive. Someone must have had a reason for killing her."

"I incline to Inspector Bracker's view, sir, that she was murdered by a burglar, whom she surprised in the act of theft."

"No sign of anything being taken."

"Chap probably panicked and got out as quickly as he could after hiding her body under the bed."

"Though, now you mention it," Chudd went on, "there was only some loose silver in her handbag. There weren't any bank notes."

"And there certainly isn't any money in the house. We've been right through everything again this morning."

"Any sign of the spare front-door key?"

"No. I don't believe Miss Dunkley ever left it there as she says."

"And what inference do you draw from that?"

Sergeant Roberts pursued his lips. "Nothing in particular. There could be a perfectly innocent explanation."

"You don't think it of possible significance that the person who had a motive and who had opportunity has also conceivably told a lie about leaving her door key when she departed?"

Sergeant Roberts was thoughtful for a time. "Frankly, sir, I just don't believe the Dunkley woman did it."

"That's what your personal computer throws up?" Chudd asked with a quizzical gleam.

"That's about it, sir."

"Is it known to give you wrong answers?"

Sergeant Roberts grinned. "It's about as accurate as the weather forecasts."

Chudd picked up a sheet of paper from his desk and read it.

"No recent Borstal or Approved School escapees who might have headed our way, I note," he remarked.

"We've also accounted for all our known thieves and housebreakers," Roberts added. "So if it was a burglar, it was either a novice or an outsider."

"I suppose Mrs. Hibbert's house might be regarded as respectable prey?"

"I don't think there's any doubt about that, sir. You wouldn't find the big-time gangs or the professional jewel thieves making a set at it, but it's just the sort of property to attract the attentions of the nuisance burglar. Nuisance from our point of view, I mean. Nothing much is taken because there isn't a great lot to take, but it thoroughly upsets the householder, sets us off on another hopeless trail and leaves everyone disgruntled. Meanwhile, the chap has drifted on, broken a few more kitchen or bathroom windows and had further pickings."

"There's no evidence this house was broken into," Chudd reminded him.

"He could have gained access by knocking on the door, pretending to be a salesman, or from one of these queer religious sects, which are active nowadays. Something of that sort."

"Nobody else appears to have seen such a person in the street," Chudd said, doubtfully.

"It could have been dark. Anyway do we know for certain whether Mrs. Hibbert kept the doors locked even when she was in? I'm thinking in particular of the side-door."

"So am I. It's something I should have asked Miss Dunkley. We'll go and see her now."

Chudd reckoned they would catch her during the school lunch break, and sent Sergeant Roberts to find her while he sat in the car which was thoughtfully parked round a corner out of view of the main entrance. He could see from her expression as she approached, however, that their visit was far from welcome.

Roberts opened the rear door and she got in, saying as she did so, "This is extremely inconvenient and I really must ask you not to come hanging around the school. It looks terrible."

"I'm sorry but I wanted to see you," Chudd replied firmly. "Anyway, this doesn't resemble a police car so why should anyone guess what company you're keeping? But if you like we'll drive further on."

"I have to be back in twenty minutes. I have a class at two." Her tone was petulant, as well as annoyed. "What is it you want now? I thought I answered all your questions last night."

Chudd felt he had put up with enough from Miss Dunkley. "Your personal convenience means nothing to me when I'm looking for a murderer, and when, moreover, I think you may be able to help me find him."

"I don't know how I can help you further," she said, in a tone turned sulky.

"Let's see! Can you tell me first whether Mrs. Hibbert normally kept cash in the house?"

"She always had money in her handbag."

"What sort of sums did she usually carry about?"

"Once when she was ill in bed, I cashed a cheque for her at the bank. It was for ten pounds."

"But would she usually have banknotes in her handbag?"

"As far as I know, yes. She never seemed to be short of ready money."

"You don't know whether she kept a reserve in the house?"

"No idea. Occasionally there'd be the odd pound lying around on a table or under an ornament. But I never saw any large sums. I wouldn't have."

"Now, I want to ask you something about the doors. Were they usually kept locked?"

"The front-door, as you know, has a Yale lock and the catch was always kept down. As to the side-door, that also has a Yale lock. It was always locked at night and if she went out. Otherwise the latch was usually kept up."

"You mean not locked?"

"Yes."

"Was anyone in the habit of entering the house without knocking?"

"Some of the regular delivery people used to open the door and put the stuff on the kitchen table. And the man who used to come and wind the clocks always let himself in and out."

"You mean someone used to call specially to wind the clocks?" Sergeant Roberts asked incredulously.

"Yes. Do you know how many there are in that house? Twelve! That's an average of two per room including the bathroom. A man used to come and do them every Saturday morning."

Chudd experienced a sudden quickening of interest. "What man?"

"I only knew him as Arthur. He came from that little clock repair place in the High Street, two doors past Woolworth's."

Peggy Dunkley glanced at her watch. "I must get back or my class will be kicking its heels. Do you think you'll want to see me again?"

"More than likely."

"Well, try and keep away from the school. As it is, one or two of my more amiable colleagues are expecting to see me taken off in handcuffs any moment."

Despite her size, she got out of the cramped back seat of the car with surprising ease and hurried off with a long, loping stride.

"She walks like an Irish Wolfhound," Sergeant Roberts remarked, as he stared after her retreating figure.

Chudd grunted. His mind was focused on clocks rather than on the canine resemblances of Peggy Dunkley's walk.

"Is it your recollection," he asked, "that all the clocks in Mrs. Hibbert's house are going?"

"Every bloody one of them."

"I want to check that." A quarter of an hour later, he had satisfied himself of the fact. "You realise what this means?"

A sudden light dawned in Sergeant Roberts' eyes. "That the chap must have come and wound them last Saturday?"

"When, according to present assumptions, Mrs. Hibbert was already dead."

"Hmm, something needs explaining."

"And without delay."

4

LIKE most suburban High Streets, Elwick Common's had altered out of all recognition over the past thirty years. The process of change had begun before that with the arrival of Woolworth's and Marks and Spencer's and of a few of the smaller chain stores. Then had come the war in which whole stretches of the street had been devastated, so that the new planners who followed in its wake were able to enjoy a free rein with their ideas of broad pavements and service roads and shop fronts of functional inelegance. But with the advent of the supermarket came yet further changes, the most noticeable of which was the disappearance of the small shopkeeper who had been either bought, or squeezed, out of business. With him went the last vestiges of personal service, his place being taken by chits of girls to whom the customer was someone to be treated with casual indifference or, better still, ignored altogether.

One survivor, however, was "George Mundy and Son, clock and watch repairs, and restorations," whose premises stood out like a home-grown apple in a bowl of shining artificial fruit.

Mr. Mundy's head was bent over a desk, on which lay a disembowelled watch, when Chudd and Sergeant Roberts entered. The ping of the shop-door bell caused him to look up. He said nothing, however, and waited with a courteous expression for his visitor to explain the reason for his call.

"Is a man named Arthur employed here?"

"Yes, indeed."

"Is he a clock winder?"

"Amongst other things, yes. It's not a full-time occupation these days. In fact it's a dying one." He gave Chudd a half-apologetic smile. "Would you be the police by any chance?"

"As a matter of fact we are. Were you expecting us?"

"Shall we say that I'm not altogether surprised by your visit. I've read of Mrs. Hibbert's death and I know you cast your net wide in such cases. Arthur's just slipped out for a minute or two, but he'll be back almost immediately. He's only gone for a packet of biscuits."

"What's his full name?"

"Stack. Arthur Stack. I'm afraid you'll find him rather upset. Mrs. Hibbert's death has come as a great shock to him. He used to go and set her clocks every week and he regarded her very much as one of his old faithfuls. And there aren't very many left nowadays."

"Did he go last Saturday?"

"Every Saturday," Mr. Mundy replied, unctuously.

"Has he said anything to you of his visit last Saturday?" Chudd enquired.

"He's been too upset to talk about it and I haven't wished to press him for details." A practical gleam entered Mr. Mundy's eye. "Can you give me the name of the solicitor handling her estate, as I mustn't forget to submit my account?"

Before Chudd had time to do so, however, the shop-door let out another sharp ping and Mr. Mundy said, "Ah, here's Arthur now."

Arthur Stack stopped short when he saw the officers, and looked anxiously at his employer.

"These gentlemen are police officers, Arthur. They've called to have a word with you. Perhaps you'd like to take them into the back room where you won't be disturbed. Give me the biscuits first, though."

Stack appeared mesmerised by the three pairs of eyes resting on him. Then holding out the packet of biscuits to Mr. Mundy like a baton in a relay race, he lunged through the curtained doorway at the rear of the shop, followed by the two officers. Chudd reckoned that he was in his mid-thirties, possibly nearer forty. His hair was black and was brushed straight back from his forehead. From behind, an oval of scalp shone

49

through like a wax seal. He had a long face and his chin, which had a strangely pendulous appearance, gave every impression of being the seat of his emotions.

The room in which they now found themselves had a low ceiling and a window which looked out on to a blank wall. A work bench was littered with clocks and watches in varying states of dismemberment. There were two ancient wooden chairs against a wall and these Stack offered to his visitors, seating himself on a music stool over by the work bench.

"What can I do to help you, gents?" he enquired in a nervous tone.

"We're investigating Mrs. Hibbert's death. I gather from Mr. Mundy you already know of it," Chudd said.

Stack nodded eagerly. "Didn't half give me a shock when I read about it in last night's paper. One of the best was Mrs. Hibbert," he went on impulsively. "Took a bit of knowing, but a real lady she was. Don't often meet her likes nowadays."

It occurred to Chudd that Stack and his employer almost overdid their lamentation for what they obviously regarded as the more spacious days of an earlier era. One in which clock-winding could be a full-time occupation.

"I believe you called at her house last Saturday?" Chudd said casually.

"That's right. Never missed except the two Saturdays when I was on holiday."

"What time would that have been?"

"Must have been around eleven-thirty."

"And how did you get in?"

Stack passed his tongue across his lips. "Through the side-door. It was usually unlocked. Mrs. Hibbert used to leave it like that when she knew I was coming and then I could enter without disturbing her. Also, she was a bit deaf. Wouldn't admit to it, mark you, but she was."

"And what did you do after you'd entered the house?"

"Started on the clocks."

"Did you see anyone while you were there?"

"Only Mrs. Hibbert."

"You saw Mrs. Hibbert!" Chudd ejaculated.

Stack's chin began to quiver with animation. "Naturally I saw her," he said excitedly.

"Where?"

"It must have been in the drawing-room."

"Why *must have been*?"

"Well, that's where I did see her."

"And what was she doing?"

"Doing?" he echoed in an agitated voice. "I think she was reading."

"What?"

"The newspaper. That's right, I remember now, she was reading the newspaper."

"Are you sure?"

"It might have been a magazine."

"Are you quite certain you saw her at all?" Chudd waved him into silence and went on, "You see, Mr. Stack, the medical evidence indicates that she was dead on Saturday morning. Are you really saying that you saw her alive? Think very carefully before you answer."

Stack had jumped up while Chudd had been talking and was taking short, nervous paces within the confined limits of the room.

"It'll be much easier if you sit down and keep calm," Chudd added.

"Keep calm when that dear old lady lies murdered! I haven't been so upset since my own sweet mother's death."

Chudd threw Sergeant Roberts a long-suffering glance. "Well, what's the answer to my question?"

Stack gulped. "Of course I saw her on Saturday. How could I be mistaken about a thing like that! I couldn't be, could I?"

"And you're absolutely positive she was in the drawing-room, reading?"

"That's right."

"Did you speak to her?"

"Just passed the time of day like."

"Try and remember the exact words you used."

"I don't really recall exactly what I said. I mean I had no special reason to."

"No, but this was an old lady of whom you were particularly fond, so I'd have expected you to have some detail of the conversation still in mind."

"I asked her how Nero was."

"And?"

"She said he was all right."

"What else?"

Stack scratched his head. "I believe I told her that I was going to the football match on Saturday afternoon and she said she wasn't interested in football."

"Anything else?"

"That was about all."

"How long were you at the house?"

"Best part of half an hour. There are twelve clocks to see to and some of 'em need a bit of regulating."

"Did you enter Mrs. Hibbert's bedroom?"

"Yes, same as I always do. There's a clock in there which has to be wound."

"Notice anything while you were in her bedroom?"

"What you getting at?"

"Don't worry your head about what I'm getting at, just answer the question."

"No, I didn't notice anything particular about her bedroom. It was just ordinary like it always was."

"And did Mrs. Hibbert remain in the drawing-room all the time you were in the house?"

"As far as I know she did."

"And did you speak to her again before you left?"

"Just to say good-bye like."

"And which door did you go out by?"

"Same as I come in by."

"Leaving it unlocked?"

"No, I slipped the catch."

"Why?"

"Because . . . . er . . . because Mrs. Hibbert asked me to."

His mouth worked like a rabbit's. "Said she might take a nap before lunch and so would I let the catch down."

"You're sure of that?"

"Couldn't be mistaken, could I?"

"Not genuinely mistaken, no," Chudd agreed. "Did you notice anything on the hall table?"

"Didn't have any cause to."

"But there's a grandfather clock beside it, didn't you notice what was on the table when you were winding the clock."

"'Fraid not."

"You didn't observe whether there was an airmail letter waiting to be posted."

"No."

"Or a key lying there?"

"No."

"Or a newspaper?"

"Can't help you. I'm afraid," he replied almost jauntily, as though he felt he could now see the end of his ordeal.

"From what you say, you must have been the very last person to have seen Mrs. Hibbert alive," Chudd said, eyeing him with quizzical interest. He rose. "I'd be obliged if you'd come down to the station so that we can take your finger-prints," he went on. "Purely a matter of routine, but you'll realise it's important to identify as far as possible all the prints we've discovered at the house. A number of them are bound to be yours."

Stack's chin quivered in renewed agitation as he nodded his head in agreement.

At the police station Chudd decided he would take advantage of its more compelling atmosphere to pursue his questioning. But first he wished to put through a call to Dr. Tracy. This, however, was more easily conceived than achieved, though he did eventually run the pathologist to earth as he was about to leave one of the public mortuaries which formed his daily circuit.

"Is it possible that Mrs. Hibbert could have been alive as late as middle day on the Saturday, Dr. Tracy?" he asked.

"You have a special reason for asking, I gather?"

"I have. Namely we have a witness who says he saw her alive around that time."

"A witness, you say?" There was a certain wariness in the pathologist's tone.

"May I put it this way, if you concede this as a possibility, then he *is* an important witness. On the other hand if you exclude it as such, then he automatically becomes a lying witness and I'd want to know why."

"I follow. Indeed, I had guessed as much." There was a long pause before Dr. Tracy said thoughtfully, "I estimated she had died either Friday night or early Saturday morning. Supposing we say four a.m. at the latest for early Saturday morning, supposing we then add six hours more for some freak condition of which there was certainly no evidence, that brings us to ten a.m. And you're asking whether she might have been alive another two hours after that," he went on in a ruminating voice. "My answer is no."

"What would be the latest you would give it?"

"Four a.m."

"And . . . er . . . . would you feel prepared . . . er . . ."

"To stick to that in the witness box?" Dr. Tracy interrupted. "Of course I should. I'm not given to changing my opinion as radically as that – provided some wholly new and unforeseen factor doesn't suddenly crop up."

"What sort of factor do you have in mind?" Chudd asked in a puzzled voice.

"Provided the body hadn't been removed and kept for some time in a wildly different temperature from that existing in the bedroom. Something of that sort."

"I think we can rule that out."

"I agree there's no evidence to suggest it, in which event you have my answer."

"In which further event I have a lying witness on my hands," Chudd murmured to himself as he put down the receiver. "But why should he have lied?"

He felt in his pocket for his pipe and frowned. Now where'd

he left it! He remembered taking it out, but not actually lighting it when they'd been in the back room of George Mundy's shop. He assumed that he must have put it down amongst all that clutter on the repair bench. It was in a mood of self-disgust when he turned as Sergeant Roberts ushered Stack into his office.

"We've taken his fingerprints, sir, and his statement's being typed now. It should be ready for signature in about ten minutes."

Chudd nodded. "Sit down, Mr. Stack, I'd like to ask you a few more questions."

"Certainly . . . er . . . Superintendent . . ."

"Chief Inspector."

"Yes, go ahead, Chief Inspector, I want to help you all I can. I've got nothing to hide. Murder's a nasty business. Specially the murder of an innocent old lady."

Chudd let him finish, gazed at him in a meditative sort of way and said, "The medical evidence rules out the possibility of Mrs. Hibbert having been alive when you called to wind the clocks on Saturday morning. What have you to say about that?"

For a moment Stack looked as though he was going to topple sideways and instinctively Sergeant Roberts took a quick step toward him, but then he gripped the sides of the chair and sitting bolt upright said in a voice which sounded uncomfortably parched: "Course she was alive, I've told you I spoke to her."

"I don't believe you."

"Tell me why should I invent a wicked thing like that?"

"One reason could be that you killed her," Chudd shot at him.

Stack shook his head as though not believing what his ears had heard. "Me kill her! You must be mad. I wouldn't murder anyone, certainly not an innocent old lady. Anyway, I had no motive to kill her." With an upsurge of spirit, he added, "Tell me what motive I had, if you think I done her in."

This, Chudd realised, was his weakness. He hadn't as yet found a motive, though if the evidence could be strengthened against Stack, that wouldn't worry him. Motiveless murders were not unknown. He'd check on Stack's mental background. A history of nervous disorder would provide the missing clue: moreover, he did give the appearance of someone who might be prone to bouts of erratic behaviour.

Aloud he said, "I've no idea what motive you may have had, but I shall make it my business to find out, since I'm convinced you're lying when you say you saw Mrs. Hibbert alive."

"If she wasn't alive when I was there, how could I have killed her?" Stack demanded in a sudden triumph of logic.

"You could have killed her earlier. Sometime during the night."

"I couldn't have. I was at home all Friday evening. My wife can prove that. We went to bed around eleven and I got up as usual at half-past six."

Chudd's face broke into a sudden smile. "Look, Mr. Stack, I don't really believe you did kill her. I think you do want to help our enquiries just as you say, but you're not being helpful, you know, when you persist in this lie about seeing her alive. Now, let's have the truth and carry on from there."

His tone had been sweetly reasonable, but there was no answering flicker from the other side of the desk where Stack sat in a state of apparent pertification.

"It's the truth what I've told you," he said dully. "I did see her. I did see her." It was almost as though he were trying to convince himself by repetition.

"You can't have done," Chudd replied, shaking his head.

"Go on," Sergeant Roberts broke in. "Tell us the truth. It'll be a weight off your mind."

"I have told the truth."

Chudd could see that fear was being replaced by stubbornness and that if he wasn't adroit, they would soon be reduced to a *you-did-I-didn't* dialogue. But how to find the key to Stack's conscience. Years of interrogating criminals had convinced Chudd that everyone had the primitive urge to confession, to unburden the mind, whatever the motive might be, whether it was to achieve relief or to satisfy a latent streak of exhibitionism. The interrogator's problem never varied and consisted of finding the appropriate button and pressing it.

"Shall I tell you what I think happened?" he went on after a pause. "I believe you found Mrs. Hibbert dead in the drawing-room when you went to the house and that you panicked and lost your head, and carried her body upstairs and concealed it beneath the bed. Isn't that what happened?"

"How could I do such a thing! I keep on telling you she was alive."

"And I shall keep on telling you she couldn't have been," Chudd's tone took on a note of exasperation. "Can't you see that I'm giving you every chance to tell the truth now. It's bound to come out in the end, but the longer it takes, the worse it could be for you."

And so it continued for another half hour with cajolery, threats and sweet persuasion, but with Stack maintaining his stand, nervously yet stubbornly. It was a process common enough in the investigation of crime, though one which the time-honoured Judges' Rules failed to recognise in their mutually conflicting objectives of enabling the police to conduct an effective interrogation and protecting the suspect from undue pressure.

When Stack had finally been allowed to go, Chudd found he had a splitting headache. Nor was his condition improved by the sudden return of Detective Inspector Bracker from the Court of Criminal Appeal. Before he ever reached the first floor where the C.I.D. offices were situated, Chudd was aware of his being in state of rampant fury. A few seconds later, bursting through the open doorway, he said in a tight, angry voice, "Do you realise they let those something bastards out!"

"All three?"

"All flipping three."

"On what grounds?"

"Hah!" It seemed as though Bracker's feelings were going to choke him, and it was only with difficulty that words came. "On the grounds that the perishing judge misdirected the jury on corroboration. It was all just a lot of playing with words, that's what really riles me. The odds are that most of the jurors weren't listening to him anyway at that moment and those that were probably never understood what he was trying to say. And yet the C.C.A. can say that three of the biggest villians shall go free because a judge puts his words the wrong way round. And look what he's paid, too! If I had my way, they'd stop his salary for the days he was trying that case. Here, we dash round like blue-arsed flies to arrest these people. We work longer hours than the bloody lawyers, we're up whole nights on end, we get shot at by the criminals, sniped at by the public. And what's the end of it all! We're back where we started, with our ulcers a bit nearer busting and the criminals that much cockier."

In the pause which followed this tirade, Chudd stared at him without any indication of his own thoughts. Then he said, "I suggest you go and have a cold beer."

After Bracker had gone out, he swallowed a couple of aspirin and put through a call to his home.

"Kate?"

"Hello, darling, where are you speaking from?"

"The station."

"When'll you be home?"

"God knows. Not till late, I'm afraid. How've things been today?"

"Quiet."

"David go off to school all right this morning?"

"Mmm. No troubles to-day."

"Andrew and Timmy back from school?"

"Timmy is. He brought a new friend home to tea."

"Nice?"

"Not very. I know it's not a pleasant thing to say about someone else's nine-year-old, but he struck me as a sly boy."

"Probably won't last. The friendship, I mean."

"Oh, I'm not worried. How's the enquiry going?"

"Still plodding."

"I hope you get a lead soon, Peter."

"So do I."

"I imagine it's particularly important, this being your first murder case since you arrived in the division."

"Added to which, Superintendent Manton being away."

"I see Andrew coming down the street now."

"O.K. I must go too. Remind the boys they still have a father."

"That's not necessary yet. Incidentally, did you ring for any special reason?"

"Yes, to hear your voice."

"Crikey, fancy still being in love with your wife at his age," Police Cadet Temple thought to himself as he disconnected the call which he had listened to with casual interest on the switchboard.

Chudd decided to go and see Peggy Dunkley again. He was like a dog trying to pick up a scent and re-passing constantly over the same ground in the endeavour. He found her at her new lodgings, though she was quick to point out that she had to return to the school later in the evening for a rehearsal of the orchestra in which she played the oboe.

"I shan't keep you long, Miss Dunkley," Chudd reassured her, as they entered Miss Smith's front room, which had a strong smell of furniture polish. North Avenue was certainly a comedown after Cresta Drive. "I wondered if you could help me about Stack, the clock-winding man?"

"In what way help you?"

"How did he get on with Mrs. Hibbert?"

"As well as anyone ever got on with her, so far as I'm aware."

"Did Mrs. Hibbert speak about him to you?"

Peggy Dunkley frowned impatiently at the floor. "Don't recall her doing so. He just used to come on Saturday mornings and that was all. More often than not I was out and didn't see him. You're not suggesting that he had anything to do with her death, are you?"

"No, just seeking information. In particluar, trying to find out about everyone who called regularly at her house. Frankly, I feel you must be able to help me more if you really try."

Peggy Dunkley immediately bridled. "I've already given you all the assistance I can at considerable personal inconvenience – oh, I haven't forgotten that you're not concerned with my personal inconvenience! – and I don't know what more you expect me to do."

Chudd ignored the outburst. "It's a curious thing that your front-door key has never been found. Are you sure you left it on the hall table?"

"As sure as I am that you're sitting in this room," she replied without hesitation.

Chudd gazed at her with a thoughtful expression. If she had removed the key, she certainly wouldn't still have it in her possession after realising its significance.

But if she hadn't left it as she described, then he had two lying witnesses on his hands. And of those two, Peggy Dunkley undoubtedly attracted the greater suspicion. She had a motive and she had had opportunity. He decided to put the position plainly to her. Let the realities be clearly staked and her reaction recorded!

Before he could speak, however, she fixed him with the expression a hockey goalkeeper might reserve for an opposing forward and said, "Look, Chief Inspector, I know it's your job not to accept everything you're told. Moreover, your questions have made it fairly obvious that I come somewhere within your range of suspects, however fantastic that may seem to me. Nevertheless, I can't help you further about the key. I did leave it on the hall table. And I haven't tried to hide from you my annoyance at the way I was thrown out by Mrs. Hibbert. So within the time-honoured formula of the detective story, I had a motive and an opportunity. But I presume it's within your experience that suspicion does frequently point to the wrong person, does incriminate the innocent – it certainly does in school life – and I hope it won't take much longer for you to be satisfied that I had absolutely nothing to do with Mrs. Hibbert's death. Meanwhile, I suppose I must go on answering your questions with as much patience as I can muster, but please disabuse your mind of any idea that you'll be able to catch me out or break me down. You won't, because I have nothing over which to be caught out and . . . well, I'm not the sort of person who'd break down even if I had committed a murder."

Chudd raised one eyebrow quizzically. "That's an odd observation to make. If you've never committed a murder how do you know you couldn't be broken down, as you put it?"

"Because I know myself well enough to be able to say."

"But surely it's an assertion one can only base on personal experience?"

"I don't wish to be drawn into a dialectical discussion," she said tartly.

"No, but I'm interested in what you said about yourself," Chudd protested.

"You're just trying to catch me out and I've already told you to forget that idea. Anyway, of course everyone can say how he'd react to given circumstances. I've never been to the top of the Eiffel Tower, but I know quite well that I should be filled with suicidal urges if I ever did. I know that because I have an intense fear of heights."

"I wouldn't have thought you were a person with any fears."

"There isn't such a person. But the point is I know what mine are and, perhaps, more important what I'm not afraid of." She threw Chudd a challenging look as she went on, "And I haven't yet come across a fellow creature who was able to intimidate me. Frustrate, thwart, anger, and annoy, but not intimidate."

"Frustrate, thwart, anger, annoy," Chudd murmured. "You really do make yourself out a fighter. Doesn't anyone ever please or satisfy you?"

"Of course they do. Now you're being absurd. I suggest you leave psychology to the trained experts and stick to facts."

"I should have thought each of us needed a few rudiments of psychology in our respective jobs."

Peggy Dunkley gave an impatient shrug. "I really must be getting back to the school or I shall be late for our rehearsal."

"Can I give you a lift?"

"You can drop me off at the corner."

Afterwards, Chudd returned to the station. On his desk lay his pipe and beside it a scrawled note in Sergeant Roberts' hand which read: "Sir, Found this on the C.I.D. window sill."

He picked the pipe up and stuck it in his mouth. It seemed the safest place to keep it. A second later, however, he had to remove it in order to answer the telephone. With no great joy, he recognised the voice of Chief Superintendent Starwick, the uniform head of the division.

"How's your murder enquiry going, Chief Inspector?"

"I'm afraid we're still moving around in the dark, sir. As yet, we haven't had any firm leads at all."

"You've ruled out the woman lodger, then?"

"No, sir, not ruled out, but we certainly haven't enough evidence on which to charge her and anyway I'm far from convinced she did it. It doesn't seem like a woman's crime."

Chief Superintendent Starwick sent a scornful sniff down the line. "I wouldn't have thought it wise to work on pre-conceived notions of that sort. And from what I've heard, this Dunkley woman is a strapping games-mistress, not the dainty feminine type."

"That's so, sir, but I still don't think she did it."

"I'm not saying she did, only taking you up on your comment that it didn't seem like a woman's crime." There was a pause and then he went on, "On the face of it, it shouldn't be too difficult a case to break. Have you got anything on finger-prints yet?"

Chudd felt inclined to reply that viewed from an aeroplane, the English Channel didn't look particularly difficult to swim. He said, "Not yet, sir, but I'm hoping to hear something soon."

"Likely to get any help from the lab?"

"I'm not expecting much. I doubt whether they'll come up with a lead."

Chief Superintendent Starwick made a sound indicative of impatience. "Well, keep me informed, Chief Inspector. I shouldn't really have to 'phone you. You should come and report to me."

Chudd returned his pipe to his mouth and bit hard on the stem to relieve his feelings. So far as officers of the C.I.D. were concerned uniformed divisional Chief Superintendents came in two sorts of wrapping. Those who left them entirely to their own devices and did no more than pen their signatures to dockets already signed several times over by others lower down the line, and those who, though having no direct operational responsibility for the work of the C.I.D., insisted upon being kept informed of every item of criminal investigation. Chudd had no doubt which of the two he preferred. He was about to make a call to the fingerprint officer when the door opened and Inspector Bracker came in. He walked over to a chair, threw Chudd's raincoat, which was lying across it, on to the corner of the desk and sat down.

"I've just been through the file of statements," he announced baldly. "There's not a lead anywhere. The only person in the street who appears to have any powers of observation at all is that old girl who lives next to the deceased, and she was away for the weekend. The rest of them neither saw nor heard a thing."

"I suppose Miss Frayne's absence isn't connected with the murder in some way?"

"I don't see how."

"Quite frankly, nor do I. Just a coincidence she was away from home that weekend."

"Can't have been anything else," Bracker said grudgingly.

There was a silence whilst each officer chewed on his own thoughts. Then Bracker said with a note of undisguisable relish, "Bit tough on you if this turns out to be an unsolved crime. Let's hope the local paper doesn't make anything of it. The fact that you're new to the area, I mean, and had just been posted here from the more hum-drum life of the Yard."

Chudd was saved answering this taunt by the telephone.

"Detective Sergeant Freshfield of the Fingerprint Branch would like to speak to you, sir," Cadet Temple announced.

"Put him through."

"Sergeant Freshfield here, sir. I don't know whether it's

of great interest or not, but I thought I'd let you know straight-away that I've found a thumbprint on the folded newspaper which corresponds with the right thumb of Stack."

"Yes, thanks very much. That's of considerable interest."

"Good. Of course his prints were also on all the clocks. Otherwise the only ones so far are those of the deceased and of the woman lodger, but I haven't finished yet, and there may be others."

"Thanks again."

"Am I right in understanding that Stack has denied touching the paper?"

"He has by inference. Which means we've now caught him out in another lie."

"That's always a good sign, sir, in a murder enquiry. Means you've drawn the net a bit tighter."

Chudd was about to say that he wished he thought so but decided this would provide further fuel for Inspector Bracker's mordant satisfaction at the state of impasse which the investiga-tion had reached.

Instead he rang off with a cheerful good-bye and set about pondering the information he had just received. Was it a genuine grain of gold or merely another pebble which caught the eye because of its interesting shape? He wished he knew.

5

NOTHING further came to light during the next two days and Chudd, realising that in addition to the more recognisable public reactions to failure he was on trial amongst his own new colleagues, was beginning to experience the burden of despair. The trouble was that he couldn't think of any fresh initiative to take. The fact that no one else could either didn't make him feel any better. He was in charge of the enquiry and its momentum depended on him, and as he saw it three days after the discovery of Mrs. Hibbert's death, it was about to peter out.

The frustrating part was not that every piece of the jigsaw was missing, but that several pieces appeared to belong to a different puzzle. For example, it was certain that either Stack or Peggy Dunkley was lying and possibly both of them, but their lies – if they were lies and this particularly applied in Stack's case – didn't seem to provide any assistance in finding the murderer.

When questioned about his fingerprint on the newspaper, Stack had affected to recall that he had removed it from the mat inside the front-door and placed it on the hall table. He could give no satisfactory explanation for not having remembered this at his first interrogation.

But as Chudd observed wearily to Sergeant Roberts, "Where does it take us, anyway? If Mrs. Hibbert *was* alive when Stack called on Saturday morning, why hadn't she already taken in the paper herself? And if she was dead, as the medical evidence shows, why should he persist in his lie that she was alive?"

He had been to see Miss Frayne again to discover that Nero had now quite definitely adopted her and that she was distressed, as the police were, at having been away from home over the fatal weekend.

"I don't want you to think that I spy on my neighbours," she had said with a wry smile, "but I think my powers of observation probably are somewhat above the average. It's a matter of being interested in all that goes on around one. So many people might just as well live in dark cellars for all they notice of life."

Chudd had ruefully agreed.

On the Friday following the discovery of Mrs. Hibbert's body, he decided to break with routine long enough to give him the dubious pleasure of having breakfast with his sons. The three previous days he had left the house before they had come down, but since they were generally in bed and asleep by the time he reached home in the evenings, breakfast provided the best chance of catching a glimpse of them.

While Kate shuttled to and fro between stove and table, putting a plate of cereal in front of one and two sausages on fried bread in front of another (for David fried bread was a "must" at breakfast) and removing the remains of a boiled egg from the third, Chudd gazed at his family with a glow of affection, reflecting as he poured himself a second cup of tea that there weren't many fathers who would feel that way at breakfast time.

"I'm going to be a detective when I grow up," Timmy suddenly announced through a mouthful of cornflakes.

"They don't take skinny little twerps like you," David retorted loftily.

"I'm not skinny."

"Yes, you are."

"He won't be when he grows up and anyway you shouldn't call your brother a twerp," Kate broke in firmly.

"Why not?"

"It's not nice."

"What's wrong with it? Some politician called another a twerp the other day. I read it in the paper. It's not a filthy word like . . ."

"That's enough David," his father said sharply. "And you certainly don't want to learn your manners from politicians."

"They're the people who run the country," David said as though this clinched the argument.

"Still doesn't mean that their behaviour in public is an example for you to follow. It isn't."

"You have the rottenest manners of anyone in this house, David," Timmy said. "Doesn't he, Dad?"

David ignored this gibe as beneath contempt and dug into his fried bread. Meanwhile Andrew, who had remained silent throughout the interchange, sat back, sighed and announced that he was still hungry. He was the placid one of the trio, letting the not infrequent squabbles which broke out between his elder and his younger brother pass right over his head. On occasions he would, however, intervene on Timmy's side, thereby demonstrating a true British feeling for the underdog, regardless of where the merits lay.

"*If,*" Chudd said, "and I repeat *if* I'm able to take Sunday off, or part of it anyway, where would you like to go?"

Three answers came at once.

"Seaside," Timmy shouted.

"Changing of the Guard," Andrew called out.

"Windsor Park to watch the polo," David said in a superior tone.

"Where'd you hear about that?" his father enquired with interest.

"Abbott, he's the captain of the cricket eleven, goes almost every Sunday. He says it's jolly super. Do you know the rules, Dad?"

" 'Fraid not. The only time I've watched polo, I felt sorry for the ponies."

"Abbott says they enjoy it as much as the players."

"How does Abbott know?" Timmy asked belligerently, as he saw prospects of seaside receding under the interest generated by mention of polo.

"It's time you were all off to school," Kate said in an attempt to avoid a further outburst of furious argument. After they'd departed she took the last slice of toast and spread it slowly with butter and marmalade. "Glad you stayed for family breakfast?" she asked with a faint smile.

"It was nice to find everything back to normal," he replied. "It looks as though David really is beginning to settle down at last."

Kate nodded. "Yes, thank goodness, even if it means keeping up with the Abbotts and watching polo."

Chudd grinned. "And there doesn't seem to be much wrong with the other two. Incidentally, what about Timmy's new friend? The one you felt was a bit sly."

"I have an idea that's over already. He departed abruptly, leaving Timmy looking pink and silent. I didn't enquire what the trouble was."

Chudd glanced at his watch and rose. "I suppose I'd better be going myself."

Kate appeared to ignore his movement toward departure. "We've talked about the boys, but what about you? How are you settling down in the new job?"

He was pensive for a while before replying. Then: "They've taken me on probation," he said with rueful smile. "I didn't expect them to put out a welcome mat, and I suppose it's something that they haven't pulled the one which is there from under my feet."

"Haven't or haven't tried to?"

"Bracker won't hesitate to, I'm pretty sure of that."

"When he was passed over, they ought to have posted him to another division. It wasn't fair on you to leave him at Elwick Common. He sounds a nasty man."

"I doubt whether I'd like him even under the most favourable conditions, but he certainly has his good points. He's hard-working and a real professional of the old school.

"I can't understand why he's apparently so popular."

"It's the sort of uncritical popularity that a good many of the older, rougher-edged members of the Force enjoy. The sort who can slang their way through most situations and who look upon the young constable of today as being only one degree better than the young criminal. The worst thing against both, in the eyes of the likes of Bracker, being that they drink milk instead of beer." He moved round behind his wife's chair. "But don't worry, dear, I shan't let Bracker or anyone else throw me off my balance. Actually, this murder case may prove to be a help in that way. It's got us working together as a team early on." He bent down and kissed her. "See you some time."

He was just going out through the door when Kate called after him, "Peter, you've forgotten your pipe'"

He turned back and saw he'd left it beside his plate. "I

think I'd sooner knock ten years off my life and go back to cigarettes," he said, picking it up and thrusting it firmly into his pocket.

Soon after he had arrived in his office, there was a 'phone call from Mr. Dann.

"I thought I would let you know, Chief Inspector, that Mrs. Mellor has arrived in England. She called to see me yesterday afternoon."

"Did she say why she'd come?"

"I should have thought that was obvious. To claim her inheritance, to use an old-fashioned expression."

"Had she known that she was the chief beneficiary under Mrs. Hibbert's will?"

"She says not."

"But you don't believe her?"

"Really, Chief Inspector, you mustn't read meanings into my words which aren't there. I have no reason to disbelieve the lady."

"Where is she staying?"

"The Parkview Hotel in Gloucester Road."

"I'll get in touch with her."

"I told her you'd probably be doing so. I did give her your number." After a pause he asked, "Do you happen to know whether the coroner is yet willing to release the body?"

"Perhaps you'd like to get in touch with him yourself."

"I did so two days ago and he said the matter largely rested with you," Mr. Dann remarked drily. "It appears to be one of those situations in which the buck is passed with a rapidity to deceive the bystander's eye."

Chudd laughed. "Well, there have been one or two awkward occasions in recent years where the defence in a murder has kicked up a fuss because the victim's body had been buried before they'd had an opportunity of having it examined on their behalf."

"Do you mean to say that my unfortunate client remains without a Christian burial until you arrest someone for her murder! What happens if the crime goes unsolved?"

"It's all a question of what is reasonable. Obviously one can't delay for ever."

"I should hope not. I confess the whole position strikes me as being utterly macabre."

"Did Mrs. Mellor enquire about the funeral?" Chudd asked.

"Naturally. I told her it wasn't yet possible to make the arrangements. That it depended on the police."

"Was she upset?"

"I can't pretend she was. But she was still in a state of bemusement following my cable and a jet flight across the Atlantic. She may react more vigorously when she has become reorientated. Anyway, why don't you telephone her yourself, Chief Inspector?"

"I'll do so right away."

It occurred to Chudd after he'd rung off that the solicitor had adopted a curiously detached, one might almost say reserved, attitude in regard to Jessie Mellor. Perhaps the reason for this would become apparent after he had spoken to her himself.

His first surprise on doing so was her voice. He had expected to hear one which he connected with the continent of North America, though for aught he knew it might be that of a Californian or an Ontarian. Mrs. Mellor's voice, however, sounded almost as English as his own with just a slight broadening of the vowels. She made no demur at his suggestion of visiting her immediately, and said she would wait at the hotel until he arrived. Indeed, her whole attitude and manner on the telephone befitted someone who had chosen a private hotel in Kensington at which to stay.

Since Detective Sergeant Roberts was giving evidence in a case at the Magistrates' Court that morning, Chudd decided to take one of the young detective constables with him. He was about to leave his office when the telephone went.

"Detective Sergeant Skeffington at the Yard, here, sir. You wanted some enquiries made in Toronto about a woman named Jessie Mellor."

"That's right."

"We've just had something through from the R.C.M.P. The bit which may interest you, sir, is to the effect that in nineteen fifty-two she was sentenced to eighteen months for forgery of cheques."

"That's certainly very interesting. I was just off to see the lady. I'm glad you caught me before I left."

A few minutes later Chudd and Detective Constable Embler were being driven through the chaotic cross-currents of mid-morning traffic en route for Kensington.

Used though he was to the most confirmed criminals often looking like benign uncles and aunts, Chudd received a further shock on coming face to face with Jessie Mellor, who received them in one corner of the empty hotel lounge and immediately ordered coffee.

She had attractive iron-grey hair with a soft wave, and her slightly sunburnt face bore a serene and calm expression. She was wearing a plain dark blue dress, stylishly set off by a multi-coloured chiffon scarf round her neck. To Chudd, she resembled a top female executive; one of the new breed of women bank managers or possibly even a lady judge.

"I gather you hadn't seen your cousin, Mrs. Hibbert, for a considerable number of years," Chudd said, after a brief exchange of pleasantries.

"That is so, Mr. Chudd. Cousin Florence and I last met shortly before the war when I was over here on a short visit."

"How long have you lived in Canada, Mrs. Mellor?"

"I went there with my parents in nineteen-thirty and have lived there ever since."

Was it possible that this poised and obviously intelligent woman had seen the inside of prison? Chudd asked himself in surprise. Surely there was a mistake somewhere.

Mrs. Mellor poured out the coffee, and with the air of a gracious hostess handed cups to her two visitors.

"There are one or two matters connected with Mrs. Hibbert's death which are puzzling us and which you may be able to help us over," Chudd said, putting his cup down on the table. "I first should like to ask you this. Had you

71

plans to visit this country before you heard of her death?"

Mrs. Mellor gave a small, deprecating smile, which was accompanied by a helpless flutter of one of her hands.

"My cousin had been very anxious for me to come over and was doing her best to persuade me to commit myself to a trip."

"And had you?"

She let out a short laugh. "Well, I guess I had really. I said I'd come over in the fall, but I'm not sure that I would have, even though I had made a reservation."

"Was there ever any question of your coming *this* month?"

"You mean before I heard of my cousin's death?"

"Yes."

"No, never." Her tone was puzzled. "Do you have some reason for asking that?"

"As you may know, Mrs. Hibbert had a lodger, a schoolmistress called Miss Dunkley. A few days before her death she gave Miss Dunkley extremely short notice to get out on the grounds that she required her bedroom for you."

"For me!" Mrs. Mellor's tone sounded full of surprise. "Miss Dunkley must be mistaken. My cousin certainly wasn't expecting me this month, so why should she pretend so to this schoolmistress person?"

"It's one of the matters which has been puzzling us," Chudd said with a sigh. "Did Mrs. Hibbert ever mention Miss Dunkley in any of her letters to you?"

"She may once or twice have made some incidental reference to her, but that was all. In fact I don't think I even knew her name until you said it just now. She simply referred to her as 'my lodger'. I certainly never received the impression that she played any significant part in my cousin's life, if that's what you're really asking."

Chudd didn't indicate whether this was what he was really asking or not, but moved on to his next question. He was a police officer collecting information and as such would only openly react for a specific purpose, usually to extract a bit more.

"Can you tell me something about Mrs. Hibbert's family. I gather you're her nearest living relative, is that right?"

"I think it probably is," Mrs. Mellor replied thoughtfully. "She did have a sister who died about fifteen years ago. I know that because when we began corresponding she asked if I remembered her sister and mentioned her death in a motor accident."

"Was this sister married?"

"Yes. Her husband, who was driving the car, was killed, too."

"What was their name?"

"I'm afraid I don't know that. I don't think my cousin ever mentioned it and, of course, Amy – that's the sister – married after I left England."

"Was she older or younger than Mrs. Hibbert?"

"Six or seven years younger." Mrs. Mellor appeared to be making some calculation. "I believe she became married during the war and she must have been in her mid-thirties then."

"Were there any children?"

Mrs. Mellor frowned and shifted in her chair. "Well, yes, there was. A little boy. He can't have been more than five when his parents were killed."

"And what happened to him?"

Mrs. Mellor looked up and met Chudd's gaze full on. "I've no idea. My cousin never mentioned him at all in any of her letters."

"How do you know of this existence then?"

"She just mentioned him the once in reference to her sister's death. She said she wasn't able to do anything for the child and I gathered he was in some sort of an institution. Perhaps I ought to mention that my cousin and her sister never got on awfully well when they were younger. Of course I can't speak of the years while I've been in Canada."

"Did Mrs. Hibbert ever mention where this accident, in which her sister was killed, took place?"

"No."

"It could be important, would you think hard for a moment."

"I don't need to. I know that she didn't. It could have been anywhere as far as I'm concerned."

"You don't definitely know it was in this country?"

"Not even that, though I assumed so. I would have expected her to have mentioned if it had happened abroad."

Chudd chewed pensively at the corner of his mouth. There was precious little to go on; moreover it could be one enormous red herring. The family background, however, couldn't be ignored, unproductive though it might subsequently turn out to be.

"I take it you're not a first cousin?" he asked suddenly.

"My mother and Mrs. Hibbert's mother were first cousins, which makes us second ones."

"And do you have brothers or sisters?"

"No. I was an only child of parents who were themselves only children."

"I'm not very clear how you and Mrs. Hibbert came to correspond with each other after several years of silence?"

"Nearly twenty years of silence," Mrs. Mellor said with a nod. "She wrote to me first. It must have been about eight years ago, shortly after her husband's death. I suppose she was lonely or perhaps I should say curious to find out what had happened to her nearest surviving relative."

"But there was this nephew," Chudd interjected.

"I've told you that I've no idea what happened to him. As far as I'm concerned he has no existence. Mrs. Hibbert has never once mentioned him." Mrs. Mellor's tone was sharp, as if she didn't wish to be reminded of the possibility that such a person did still exist.

"How did she find out where you were living in Canada?"

"She wrote to the only address she knew and the letter chased me from one place to another. It's a tribute to the Canadian postal authorities that it did ever catch up with me."

"And where were you at that time?" Chudd enquired.

"In Toronto, where I've been for the past fifteen years. Before that I was in Montreal. And when I first was out there, we were in Calgary. I moved east after my parents' death."

"I'd like now to ask you one or two rather personal questions."

"Gracious me, Chief Inspector, isn't that what you've been doing this last half hour!"

"*More* personal, perhaps I ought to have said."

"Well, there's no harm in your trying," she replied with a steely look in her eye, "but I can't see what any of this has to do with my cousin's death."

"We know so little about her," Chudd explained. "We're having to build up her background from scratch."

"I thought we were talking about *my* background."

"It's a common one in places."

"O.K. Let's have your questions"

"You're married?"

"Yes," she replied drily. "I married Evelyn Mellor in nineteen hundred and fifty and we were divorced in nineteen fifty-one."

"And you went to prison in nineteen fifty-two," Chudd wanted to add. Aloud he said, "And you've never remarried?"

"You're quite right. I have not."

"Will the inheritance left you by Mrs. Hibbert make a great difference to your life."

"Do I want the money?" she asked in a slightly hectoring tone. "If that's your question, yes, I do. I've had to earn my living and I'm quite ready to stop doing so."

"What sort of job have you had?"

"I've been a hotel receptionist. I've run a girl's hostel. I've been a sales attendant in a big store. I've worked in a hospital and I've been housekeeper to a millionaire. Is that enough for you to be getting along with?" she enquired sardonically.

"Did you start working immediately after your divorce?" Chudd asked.

"You're too right. I had to live and it's no easier to do it in Canada without money than anywhere else."

"I'm sorry, I didn't mean to distress you."

"I'm not distressed, just getting a trifle tired of your questions, that's all."

"I'm afraid the police are by nature importunate when it comes to seeking information."

"It seems, too, that they're not bound by any laws of relevance," she observed.

"How long are you proposing to stay in this country, Mrs. Mellor?"

"As long as is necessary to settle all that requires to be settled."

"Mr. Dann has probably told you that the funeral can't yet be held?"

"So I understand."

"And I imagine there may be delays in winding up the estate so long as the murder remains unsolved, though of course that's something outside my province."

"I gathered from Mr. Dann that he can be getting on with a number of details."

"Oh, that's fine ! I only hope you're not kept kicking your heels for too long."

"Don't worry, on occasions such as this, it's much better to be on the spot."

Chudd realised that he no longer had any difficulty in accepting that Mrs. Mellor had been in prison. There was an unmistakable steeliness in her made-up which had become apparent as the interview had proceeded.

"Could I have a look at your passport before I leave?"

She opened a large shiny black handbag on the chair beside her and took the passport out.

"It's an emergency one I got specially for the journey," she remarked in a tone in which Chudd thought he detected slight amusement. "My previous one expired some time ago. The authorities were very helpful when I explained that I had to fly to England immediately."

Chudd turned the pages slowly. The entries bore out what she had told him. The only stamp in it showed her arrival at London Airport the previous day. He returned it to her.

His mind fell to pondering a theory in which Jessie Mellor, learning of her cousin's intention of changing her will and fearing her own exclusion from it, had flown over, murdered her, flown back, destroyed her passport, obtained a new one

76

and re-crossed the Atlantic in response to Mr. Dann's cable.

Even if it had happened, heaven knew whether they'd ever be able to prove it, but since he regarded it as just within the realm of outside possibility, it became worthy of further examination. He rose, indicating that the interview was at an end and hoping that this would also help to mitigate the apparent significance of his remaining questions.

"When did you last receive a letter from Mrs. Hibbert?"

"We'd been corresponding rather more than usual recently in view of my prospective trip here in the fall. I must have had a letter from her about two weeks before her death."

"Do you still have it?"

"No, I never keep letters," she replied firmly.

"Did Mrs. Hibbert ever give you any hint that you were the chief beneficiary under her will?"

"Absolutely none! Mr. Dann's cable came as an overwhelming surprise."

"Were you expecting a legacy of any sort?"

"I never gave it a thought."

"Did Mrs. Hibbert ever mention her will in any of her letters?"

"Really, Chief Inspector! What bizarre ideas you do have! Well, of course she didn't. Any more than I referred to mine when I was writing to her."

He hadn't expected to get anywhere, nor had he. Nevertheless, his theory still remained within the realm of outside possibility and the question was how to probe it further. At the moment he could see no way of doing so, and perhaps it was silly even to contemplate the necessity. Was it too far-fetched, too elaborate for serious consideration? Put like that, there seemed to be only one answer; yes.

Making sure he had his pipe, he bade Mrs. Mellor good-bye. As they started on the return journey to Elwick Common, he turned to D.C. Embler and said, "How did she strike you?"

"Like best Aberdeen granite, sir."

"But truthful?"

D.C. Embler shrugged. "I don't think lies would bother her

very much if she thought them to be necessary and in her interest."

"I'm certain she wouldn't," Chudd remarked, and posed his theory to the young detective constable.

"It all sounds a bit too clever, sir."

"It's clever all right," Chudd agreed. "But Mrs. Mellor's a clever woman." And then because he was a painstaking worker and this was his first murder case in the division, and also because he felt Embler had brushed his theory aside a bit too readily he went on, "I want you to dig into Mrs. Hibbert's family background, find out the name of that married sister, the circumstances of her death and what's happened to the boy."

The detective constable's expression was properly impassive as he said, "I'll try, sir."

But he had a vision of himself forgotten amongst the archives of Somerset House long after the case had been solved. Detective Chief Inspectors out to earn their spurs, he decided, could become a pain in the neck. However, by the time they reached Elwick Common he had become reconciled to the task ahead and was further of the view that the new D.C.I. was going to be all right once they'd moulded him to their ways.

6

"Afternoon, Miss F."

Miss Frayne looked up from the front bed she was engaged upon weeding to see Mr. Wimbush's head framed by the laurel which stood guard at her front gate. A second later he had stepped inside.

"Heard how they're getting on?" he asked, nodding in the direction of Mrs. Hibbert's house. Without waiting for an answer he went on, "Looks to me very much as if it's going to be one of the unsolved murders. I only hope it won't depress the value of our properties."

"That would seem most unlikely," Miss Frayne replied, straightening up and brushing bits of soil off her gardening gloves.

"You can't be too sure. Remember Rillington Place where that fellow Christie lived, they had to change the name of the street it got so bad."

Miss Frayne smiled tolerantly. "I'm afraid I don't see much in common between Mrs. Hibbert and Christie's victims. I think you're exaggerating."

"You hope I am," Mr. Wimbush said in a lofty tone. Then: "Have the police been to see you?" Miss Frayne nodded. "Who was it, Detective Sergeant Roberts?"

"No, Detective Chief Inspector Chudd came to see me."

Mr. Wimbush frowned. Why had Miss Frayne merited a visit from someone two ranks up on the officer who'd called on him! Clearly a someone whose priorities were badly out of order. As a retired civil servant whose life had been devoted to the niceties of rank and protocol, he felt that he had been slighted. He consoled himself with the thought that Miss Frayne might be unaware of the relative importance of a chief inspector and a sergeant. But even this was stillborn when the next minute she said, "He's the officer in charge of the case."

"I didn't bother to find out about the man who came to see me," Mr. Wimbush said in a tone of airy dismissal. He peered around the garden. "Is her cat still with you?"

"Nero? Yes, he seems to have made himself completely at home."

"Cats are not like dogs. No feelings of loyalty. As long as they're fed, they don't mind who by. Did I ever tell you about my dog – Rambler . . . ?"

"Yes," Miss Frayne said quickly. She'd heard a good many

stories about Rambler, who formed the other topic for Mr. Wimbush's anecdotes. On the whole, Miss Frayne found his reminiscences of life in the Ministry of Transport less tedious than those centred round his faithful dog.

"Anyone been next door, apart from the police?" he asked, staring across at Mrs. Hibbert's now sealed home.

Miss Frayne shook her head. "I haven't seen anyone. I imagine the police have the keys."

"Had any news of Miss Dunkley since all this happened?"

Miss Frayne again shook her head. "No, I thought she might have been round to see me, but she hasn't. I expect she's been very busy."

"The police probably have her under suspicion," Mr. Wimbush said importantly.

"Peggy Dunkley! That's absurd! Of course she had nothing to do with it. You really ought to be more careful what you say."

He flushed under the rebuke. "If you knew as much about police work as I do," he said with a display of dignity, "you'd realise the truth of my observation. One can't ignore facts just because one finds them personally distasteful." Then having delivered himself of this little lecture, he departed, contriving to give Miss Frayne the impression that she was keeping him from more important affairs.

She returned to her weeding, but not for long since a car pulled up and Detective Chief Inspector Chudd got out. He paused inside the gate and smiled as she sat back on her heels and pointed a trowel at him.

"I'm obviously not intended to get any weeding done to-day," she remarked. "You're my second visitor in five minutes."

"On the rare occasions I'm driven to weed the garden I'm always praying for interruptions. You can't pretend you actually enjoy doing it."

"But I do," Miss Frayne exclaimed. "It's so constructive and an excellent mental therapy as well."

"I can think of less back-breaking therapy." He glanced toward the house. "May we have a word inside?"

She led the way into the sitting-room and sat down.

"I'm sorry to bother you again, but you're the only person in Cresta Drive who seems able to assist us." Miss Frayne looked appropriately pleased by this clear recognition of her sense of duty, and Chudd went on, "It's about the clock-winder who used to call at Mrs. Hibbert's every Saturday morning."

"Yes, I used to see him."

"Which door did he usually enter by?"

"The side-door. He invariably knocked and then let himself in."

"I see. What about when he left?"

"By the same door."

"Do you recall whether he usually let the catch down?" Miss Frayne looked puzzled and Chudd added, "You might have noticed the difference between merely closing the door and giving it a hard tug."

"To the best of my recollection he closed it quite normally."

"Can you say that he never slammed it as though the catch were down?"

"I can't say that he never did, but I don't remember his doing so." She cast a worried glance at the floor. "I'm sure I would have noticed if he had regularly slammed it. I'm sorry I can't be more helpful."

"On the contrary, what you've just told us is very helpful. Anything which indicates a break with normal routine is helpful." He sighed. "But what a pity you were away last week-end! You might have been even more helpful if you'd stayed at home."

"I realise that." Then carried away somewhat by the thought of what might have been if her sense of duty hadn't despatched her to look after two rampageous children she added, "To think, you might even have caught the murderer by now."

"Could be." He was on the verge of mentioning that the police had been able to clear her of suspicion when he decided that this might not be well received. At any rate he was now satisfied that Miss Frayne's absence over the weekend was not directly linked with Mrs. Hibbert's death. Satisfied, that is, until something turned up to cause him further reflection.

"I suppose you've seen Peggy Dunkley?" Miss Frayne now asked.

"Several times."

"How is she? Is she getting over the shock of it?"

"She gives the impression of being more annoyed than shocked."

"Poor Peggy! She'd make some man a wonderful wife. I do hope I didn't give you a wrong picture of her when you were here before. She's really an awfully kind person and she was very good to Mrs. Hibbert, too, in various ways."

"What ways?"

Miss Frayne appeared flustered. "Well . . . like doing jobs about the house. She could mend fuses and she once papered one of the rooms."

"Her own bedroom?"

"I believe it was . . . but it still showed what a kind heart she possessed. Anyway, Chief Inspector, I don't want you to get the idea that Peggy and Mrs. Hibbert were always at each other's throats . . ." Her hand flew up to her mouth. "Oh, dear, what an unfortunate expression I've used! What I mean is, they weren't constantly at loggerheads or anything of the sort."

"It's quite all right, Miss Frayne," Chudd said. "Nothing you've told me has weighed against Miss Dunkley by itself. No one has suggested that they were always on bad terms or threatening one another with violence, but the fact remains that Mrs. Hibbert was killed not long after they'd had a particular row and on the very day that Miss Dunkley was forced to leave."

"What can I say to persuade you that Peggy couldn't possibly have murdered her? I know she couldn't have."

Chudd smiled as he might have at a worried child. "Leave the facts to do their own persuasion," he said drily. "Now I'll leave you to get on with your weeding."

"I don't feel like doing it any more, now." Miss Frayne replied, her expression clouded by uncertainty. "I feel I've let Peggy down and you're taking advantage of it."

"Stop fretting. You've done no more than your duty required of you."

"I hope so," she said, clutching at the proffered straw.

Chudd, whose own conscience was a fairly straightforward piece of mechanism, felt little sympathy with Miss Frayne's own agony of conscience, arising from a sense of duty which had apparently been required to do the splits.

He arrived back at the station to be informed that Deputy Commander Ellis had been on the telephone and wanted him to call back as soon as he came in. There were three Deputy Commanders in C Department at Scotland Yard, who ranked below the Assistant Commissioner, Crime (or A.C.C. as he was generally known) and the Commander who was his Second-in-Command. Two of them were in charge of Sub-departments at the Yard, the third had responsibilities for C.I.D. affairs in the Districts and Divisions in which the M.P.D. was organised. It was for the benefit of this one that Chudd now mustered his thoughts. He had always got on well with Deputy Commander Ellis who had been a Detective Inspector when he, Chudd, had been a Detective Constable. For a short period they had served in the same division and Chudd still cherished a memory of Mr. Ellis, who was six feet four in his socks and as thin as a bean pole, clambering head first through a skylight. It had seemed an eternity before his feet had finally slithered from view to be followed by a hoarse cry as about ten shillings' worth of small change complied with the call of gravity and cascaded from his pocket on to a marble floor.

"Chudd here, sir," he announced when the connection was made. "I understand you called when I was out."

"How are things going, Peter? I'd meant to come and visit you, but I just haven't been able to get away from my blasted desk this week. So give me a run down. The A.C.C. was enquiring yesterday, too."

"Well, I haven't given up hope, sir, but I confess it's pretty sticky. There're a whole lot of leads but none of them seem to take one to a murderer."

"Be more explicit."

"First there's this Dunkley woman, the lodger, who could have done it, except that there's no evidence. And there's also the unresolved mystery of her front-door key which she swears she left on the hall table but which has completely disappeared. Then there's the clock winder who insists against all evidence to the contrary that Mrs. Hibbert was alive when he called on the Saturday morning. And finally there's the mystery of the patently false reason which Mrs. Hibbert gave Miss Dunkley for asking her to leave at a few days notice. Coupled with that is the sudden appearance in this country of the cousin whom Mrs. Hibbert used as an excuse. She inherits the lion's share of the estate and I've learnt to-day that she has a conviction for forgery in Canada."

"Forgery of a will?"

"The message from the R.C.M.P. said cheques."

There was a pause before Deputy Commander Ellis said, "The Dunkley female is the link you must hammer at. It's inconceivable that she doesn't know more about why she was thrown out. She must be lying about that. After all, the cousin confirms what that letter you found says, namely, that she wasn't proposing to come until the autumn. I simply don't believe that the dead woman gave that as an excuse to be rid of Dunkley. And from that it's only a short step to questioning whether she gave her the push at all."

"On the other hand, sir, Peggy Dunkley did tell Miss Frayne, the next door neighbour, several days beforehand that she'd been asked to leave."

"Could well have been one of her acts preparatory." Then he went on, "As I see it, Dunkley had opportunity. Her motive, such as appears on the surface, is insubstantial. Lodgers don't normally commit murder because they're asked to quit, however outraged they may feel. On the other hand how do we know she didn't have some much stronger motive which she's skilfully concealing behind the apparent one? Just stop and think for a moment. We only have her word for it that she was asked to leave! We only have her word for it that Mrs. Hibbert said she needed the room for her cousin from Canada! We only have her word for it that she left her door key on the hall table." A silence followed before the Deputy Commander said, "That's right, isn't it?"

"Ye-es, it is, sir," Chudd replied slowly.

"And that's why I say you ought to hammer at that particular link. Have her along at the station and really bang that story of hers. Take her through it until she can't distinguish a tennis racquet from a boomerang."

"What do you feel about Stack, sir?"

"I'd give him hell, too."

"I have done, but he still sticks to his story."

"His lie is obviously a red herring and so you don't want to be too distracted by it. Dunkley's your target."

"I'll get her along this evening."

"Do that and let me know in the morning how it went. That is, unless in the meantime I read in my paper that you've arrested and charged her."

"I doubt that, sir. She's a tough nut."

"Then use your strongest crackers."

The Deputy Commander smothered a cough at the other end of the line and went on, "This case apart, how are you finding things, Peter?"

"Oh, I'm settling down slowly, sir."

"Expect you're finding it as different as Petticoat Lane from Fortnum and Mason's. Got many number one dockets on your plate?"

"Two, and a third one came in to-day. Allegation that a P.C. assaulted a fifteen-year-old whom he caught stealing his bicycle."

"Sounds a not unfamiliar story," Deputy Commander Ellis remarked wearily. "God knows where it's going to stop. I sometimes wonder whether the public, or certain sections of it, will be satisfied until our conversion to cannibalism is complete."

On this cheerless note, their conversation ended. Shortly afterwards Inspector Bracker barged into the room in his customary manner, as though it was his by rights and Chudd merely had temporary use of it. Deciding, however, that if he made an issue of every needling incident life would become utterly intolerable for everyone, Chudd accepted the intrusion without comment.

"Mind if I look in your cupboard?" Bracker asked at the same time as he opened it and peered along the top shelf. "Chief Inspector Gilman used to keep a pot of glue in here and I wondered if it was still around. I've just accidentally torn an original exhibit in two and thought I'd better stick it together again." He shoved a hand into the back of the cupboard. "Doesn't seem to be here any more. Someone must have swiped it. Perhaps they've got some downstairs."

"What's the exhibit?" Chudd asked.

"Bloody prisoner's statement."

"How are you going to explain that in court?"

"Just tell the beak what happened," Bracker replied airily. "I assure you that worse things than that have happened before now. We're probably not quite as fuss-bound as you fellows at the Yard. I once completely lost a bunch of skeleton keys we'd found on a man arrested for housebreaking."

"And what did you do that time?" Chudd enquired, with casual interest.

Bracker smirked. "You'd better not ask."

Chudd didn't. He could guess, anyway. Early on in his career a police officer had to decide just how far he was prepared to deviate from the strict and narrow path of duty as defined in countless regulations. A path which, if always scrupulously adhered to, would more often than not fail to lead to an arrest. Not only was the criminal of to-day intelligent and skilful as never before, but the odds became steadily more weighted in his favour. Accordingly in the daily battles of wits which took place, each officer had to decide for himself where his own sense of ethics held fast. Chudd certainly didn't regard himself as holier-than-thou – no C.I.D. officer could be that and survive in the job – and he had acted on more than one occasion in a fashion which would have left him without a leg to stand on before a disciplinary board. But the one thing he had never done was to tamper, even unmaliciously, with evidence, nor had he ever succumbed to the notorious practice of adorning his case with "verbals": of gilding the lily by attributing to the defendant some statement of oral admission.

To avoid further revelations of Inspector Bracker's scrapes with propriety, he brought him up to date on his recent discussion with the Deputy Commander. When he had finished, Bracker said, "That's exactly my view, too. Crack that Dunkley woman and we'll be a long way to solving the case. It's obvious she hasn't told us all she knows. Shall I go and fetch her now? I'd enjoy hauling her out of a gymnasium."

Chudd shook his head. "I'll send Sergeant Roberts."

"Just as you like," Bracker said with a sniff. "But I thought it'd be better if she saw we meant business. I'll tell Roberts you want her brought here."

"It's O.K. I'll tell him myself."

Inspector Bracker refrained from further comment and walked scowling out of the room.

When Detective Sergeant Roberts had been located and directed to the Detective Chief Inspector's room, Chudd said to him, "I want Peggy Dunkley brought here, but as tactfully as possible. I'd like to see her as soon as possible, but don't interrupt her in the middle of a class or anything like that. Tell her there are some further points to be gone over and I'd be obliged if she'd accompany you to the station, and suggest that that would be more convenient than at her lodgings."

"Leave it to my powers of persuasion, sir." Sergeant Roberts said cheerfully. "Not that I expect she'll make any fuss. They usually co-operate at this stage, if only grudgingly. Incidentally, may I take your car? It's the only one available."

"Sure." Chudd supposed it was thanks to television that the public was under the fond belief that police officers had waiting lines of sleek, pepped-up cars at their disposal. Nothing could have been further from the truth so far as the C.I.D. was concerned. The car which Chudd was using was allocated to the Detective Superintendent and it was only because Manton was off the division for a couple of weeks that he had a vehicle to himself. Moreover, far from being the sort of car associated in the general mind with police activity, which had a revolving blue beacon on its roof and a glittering façade of chrome accessories in front, it was a small family saloon with rattling doors and a gear lever knob that came off in your hand.

It was forty minutes before Sergeant Roberts returned with Peggy Dunkley. She entered Chudd's office, nostrils flared and mouth drawn tightly down to give her face an expression of utmost distaste. Chudd immediately rose.

"Sit over here, Miss Dunkley." He turned to Roberts. "You draw up a chair, too, Sergeant."

Peggy Dunkley waited until he had sat down again, then said testily, "What is it this time? Your colleague, acting I imagine on your orders, refused to tell me why you wished to see me. The whole situation is really getting beyond a joke and I'd be glad if you'd try and complete everything this time and then leave me to get on with my work. I can't think what else you can possibly want to know from me."

Chudd stared at her thoughtfully for several seconds. She sat with hands folded in her lap and head held high. There were little patches of colour on her cheeks and she breathed slowly and deeply. It suddenly struck Chudd that thirty years ago she could easily have passed for a member of the Hitler Jugend. She was dressed in a dark blue skirt and a white high-necked sweater. She had on no make-up and a signet ring on her right little finger was her only piece of jewellery, if so plain an article justified that description.

"The reason I wanted to see you," Chudd said quietly, "was because I don't believe you've told me the whole truth. I find myself unable to accept your account of what led up to your leaving Mrs. Hibbert's."

She glanced at him quizzically. "I'm sorry about that, but it happens to be the truth. And it'll still be the truth next year and the one after that. So any further questions on that subject will be a waste of your time – and mine, too. And quite frankly, it's my time that I'm more concerned about."

"What was the real reason Mrs. Hibbert gave for evicting you?"

"I've already told you several times."

"Or maybe she didn't ask you to leave at all?"

"What exactly do you mean by that?" she demanded in a tone which had a note of wariness.

"That it's a complete concoction about your being asked to leave."

"That's an absurd suggestion! Why did I leave then?"

"There could be a number of reasons."

"Give me one."

"You could have been concerned in some way with Mrs. Hibbert's death."

"*Could!* I could be planning a trip to the Pole but I'm not." She threw Chudd a scalding look. "Do I have to stay here and listen to your crazy speculations?"

"No. You can leave any time you wish. But if you do I shall inevitably draw my own inferences."

"I see. This is normal police blackmail, I suppose." She tossed her head angrily. "In the circumstances it seems I must submit to your idiotic questions."

"Good! Let's test your story a bit further."

Leaning forward, arms rested, on the desk, Chudd began his questioning in earnest. His tone remained quiet. There was nothing hectoring or bullying about his manner, merely a relentless persistence. His questions came not as flying grape-shot from a blunderbuss, but with the precision of well-aimed steel bullets. Time and again he would fire the same question in a different context in the hope of finding a vulnerable point in Peggy Dunkley's armour-plated defences. But in the end he was no wiser than he had been at the beginning. Each of them was exhausted, but his was the exhaustion of defeat. He might have been trying to split open the Rock of Gibraltar with a fire cracker.

He gazed helplessly across at Sergeant Roberts who had on several occasions thrown in his own questions from the flank. But Peggy Dunkley had remained unshaken in her account. Either she was telling the truth or she was certain her lies could never be uncovered. Of one thing, Chudd had no doubt, she would stand up to any cross-examiner who had no more material to go on than he.

"Is that the end?" She enquired.

"For the time being."

"I see," she said grimly. Then after a pause: "Can I rest assured that at least you won't bother me again unless you have something fresh to ask about?"

"I can't guarantee that."

"You mean you propose to harry me whenever it suits your purpose!"

"I'm only doing my job."

"You're still not satisfied that I've told you the truth?"

Chudd shrugged. "Only *you* know whether you have."

Peggy Dunkley stood up and let out a heavy sigh. "It seems we've reached an impasse." She turned to Sergeant Roberts. "Is there a car to take me home?"

"Yes, that'll be arranged, Miss Dunkley," Chudd said. He watched her go out of the room and continued staring at the door for a full minute after her departure. Then he, too, sighed, and let his gaze turn moodily to the window as he began to light his pipe. Well, he had adopted Deputy Commander Ellis's recommended tactic and achieved nothing more than a headache. Worse, he didn't even know what to believe now. Despite the curious features of Peggy Dunkley's story, he had never really thought of her as the murderer, but the Deputy Commander had gone some way to persuading him that her part might be a good deal more sinister than his own interpretation of her conduct indicated. And it was all a matter of individual interpretation at this juncture. His failure to press her into contradicting herself even in the smallest detail should have confirmed him in his provisional acceptance of her innocence, but this hadn't happened. On the contrary, the longer she stood up to his questioning, the greater grew his certainty that she was holding something back. But whether this was a case of the thought being father to the wish, he was at the moment in no position to judge.

With an almost reluctant gesture he pulled the growing

folder of statements toward him. The unsolved cases invariably finished up the heaviest in paper, he reflected gloomily, as he opened it in the remote hope of finding something missed. He had just begun to read through Arthur Stack's five-page statement without any further gain of inspiration when the telephone rang.

"Somebody in Bedford Prison wants to speak to you, sir," Police Cadet Temple announced in a tone which seemed to communicate a sharing of interest in this fact. There followed a number of disembodied clicks in the course of which Temple's own voice suddenly receded a thousand miles. The next moment, it boomed into Chudd's ear with the information that the call was through.

"Is that Detective Chief Inspector Chudd?" a military voice enquired at the other end of the line.

"Chudd speaking."

"This is Walls, the Acting Governor of Bedford Prison. Can you hear me all right?"

"Perfectly."

"Good, it sounded at one time as though a herd of buffalo was tearing up the line. I tell you why I've rung. We've a fellow in this prison who says he did the murder you're investigating."

7

As quickly as Chudd's interest soared, his spirits dropped. There was nothing more pestiferous than the false confession and there was hardly a murder investigation of any length to which this disruptive contribution had not been added at some stage or another, usually by a prisoner seeking either to relieve the tedium of his daily routine or to attract some vicarious rays of limelight.

"He's a chap named Ronald Sherbrook," the Acting Governor went on. "He's only a youngster, twenty to be exact. Was arrested day before yesterday by the police here and charged with being found on enclosed premises by night. Appeared before the beaks and was remanded in custody for seven days. There was another youth charged with him who's also here. Anyway, this afternoon when he was being taken back to his cell after exercise, Sherbrook was apparently boasting of all his exploits to the officer and casually threw out that he'd committed a murder. The officer didn't really believe him but thought he'd better ask him what he meant and Sherbrook said he'd strangled the old lady at Elwick Common. The matter was duly reported to me in the Governor's absence and I interviewed him myself. In fact only finished doing so just before I 'phoned. He didn't add much more, but he gave a certain amount of circumstantial detail and stuck to his story."

"What sort of youth is he?"

"Unstable as they come, according to his record. He's a Borstal boy and was out on licence at the time he was picked up. He's had psychiatric treatment and all that box of tricks. He's never been actually certified but he's described as immature and as having psychopathic tendencies. But perhaps it'd be best if you came and saw him for yourself. You're the only person who can really test his story."

Chudd looked at his watch and saw that it was half past five. "I'll come immediately. Should be with you some time after seven."

"I'll expect you."

Detective Sergeant Roberts had just returned with the car when Chudd told him the news. Bracker was out on another enquiry and he left him a message.

As they headed up the A.6 Chudd wondered whether this could really be the end of the chase or whether it would prove to be merely another buck of the roundabout.

Mr. Walls received Chudd and Sergeant Roberts in the Governor's office and immediately introduced Prison Officer Hurley, the man to whom Sherbrook had made his supposed confession.

"Thought you better hear it straight from Hurley first," Mr. Walls said in a business-like manner. "After that you can put Sherbrook through his paces. Does that suit you?"

"I suppose it's possible that I shall wish to speak to other prisoners too, depending on what Sherbrook says."

"That can be arranged."

Chudd turned to Prison Officer Hurley, who was quite a young man with a white, strained face and a pair of fierce eyes, and said, "I'd like to hear it from the very beginning."

"I'd locked a number of other prisoners in their cells and Sherbrook was the last," Hurley said. "I'd already marked him down as one of the talkative types. Anyway, I was waiting for him to go into his cell and he was hanging about in the entrance telling me what a big shot he was and how he'd once been the leader of some gang of youths and how the police spent months looking for him but he'd always been able to outwit them until eventually some girl grassed on him and he was arrested. It was the typical boastful stuff you hear from his sort, and I'd already told him twice to look sharp and get inside, but he continued to linger there and go on talking. The third time I warned him he'd be up before the Governor if he didn't step lively and it was then that he said in a bragging sort of tone, 'The Governor would fall off his chair if he knew I'd done a murder.'" Hurley swallowed and passed his tongue across his lips. "When he said that, I said, 'What'd you do, talk 'em to death?' and he said, 'If you don't believe me I can prove it.' And I asked him who he'd murdered and he said, 'the old girl at Elwick Common that's been in all the papers.' So I locked him up and came and reported the matter to Mr. Walls."

"You didn't have any further conversation with him after he mentioned the old girl at Elwick Common?" Chudd asked.

"No. I conceived it my duty to report the matter at once."

Mr. Walls nodded approvingly and took up the story. "As soon as Hurley had told me what had happened, I had Sherbrook brought before me. I told him I understood he'd confessed to committing a murder and a good deal to my surprise he said that was so. I asked him if it was true and he said it was. I may say I got the strong impression that he was enjoying every second of the interview. He looked much more like someone who'd just won an Olympic gold medal than the murderer of a defenceless old woman. I then warned him how serious it was to make false confessions and that he could be laying himself open to charges of public mischief and the like, but he just gave me a superior grin and said that the police would believe him even if I didn't."

"Did he say why he had decided to confess?" Chudd broke in.

"I asked him that," Walls said, "and his answer wasn't very convincing. It was to the effect that you'd have no hope of solving the case without his assistance."

"And that he had graciously decided to give it?"

"Exactly. I pressed him as to why he had chosen that precise moment to admit the murder and he just shrugged and said he had and that was all there was to it."

"You said on the telephone that he provided some circumstantial detail in support of his confession?" Chudd remarked.

"Yes, he did, but whether it's true or not only you can say. For example he described parts of the old lady's house and the road it was in."

"Can you tell me? It could be important when it comes to cross-checking his story."

"He said there was a gravel path up to the front door which was yellow. He said the living-room was on the left as you entered and the kitchen on the right. Oh, yes and he said there was a counterpane on her bed which hung right down to the floor so that the body was completely hidden when he pushed it underneath."

"That's certainly all correct as far as it goes," Chudd observed keenly. "Did he say why he'd killed her?"

"I should have mentioned that. I asked him, of course, and

he said he'd strangled her when she caught him rifling her bedroom drawers."

"Did he explain how he got into the house?"

"No, I didn't ask him that."

"Did he give any times?"

"No. Again I didn't ask him. Once I was satisfied his story *might* be true, I broke off the interview and telephoned you, after clearing things with the Home Office."

"He arrived here the day before yesterday, Wednesday, is that right?"

"Correct. He and this other lad, Billing, were arrested on Tuesday night, taken before the court on Wednesday and remanded in custody for seven days."

"So he's had forty-eight hours to make up his mind to confess?"

Walls nodded. "A common period of gestation in prison."

"And so far as anyone is aware, he hadn't made any earlier confessions?"

"Of this particular crime?"

"Yes."

"Not that's been reported to me. This is something you may find out from other prisoners he's consorted with, particularly Billing, his co-defendant on the present charge."

"Hmm. I wonder if I ought to see Billing first."

"That's up to you."

"Is he the same type as Sherbrook?"

Walls reached out for a folder on his desk. "Terence Billing, born eighteenth of January nineteen forty four." He switched the folder round and examined a photograph. "Looks like a rocker more than a mod." Turning it back he went on, "Was discharged from Borstal just over two weeks ago."

"What offence had taken him there?"

"Shopbreaking and larceny, six cases taken into consideration. And before that there'd been probation and approved school."

"He sounds a ripe companion for Sherbrook."

"And for the host of other twenty-year-olds we have inside

these walls. Well, which is it to be first, Sherbrook or Billing?"

Chudd plucked at his lower lip and stared in frowning thought at the floor. Then looking up he said, "Let's have Billing. If we know what he has to say, it may help us when it comes to listening to Sherbrook."

A few minutes later, Billing was brought into the Governor's office by a Chief Prison Officer. He was dressed in a pair of tight jeans and a black leather windcheater. His expression was compounded of wariness and surprise as he glanced at the occupants of the room. Physically, he was a well set-up youth, Chudd decided. Rather different from the run of weedy, stooping, flat-footed lads he was used to dealing with in connection with crimes of the sort Billing had committed. Though no one could call him good-looking, he had about him a certain air of virility which probably ensured him a sequence of ready girl-friends.

"Sit down, Billing," Mr. Walls said. "This is Detective Chief Inspector Chudd of the Metropolitan Police who has some questions to ask you."

Billing turned his head to give Chudd an appraising stare. Then he sat down carefully, as though he rather expected the chair to collapse beneath him.

"What is it you want to know?" he asked, the wariness of his whole attitude reflected in his voice.

"I want to ask you some questions about Sherbrook."

Billing frowned. "I don't know anything about him."

"When did you first meet him?"

"Last Monday."

"In what circumstances?"

"In a cafe near Elstree. I'd never seen him before and we just happened to get into conversation."

"What did he tell you about himself?"

"Can't remember now."

"Of course you can remember."

"Can't."

"Did he tell you where he'd come from?"

"Why not ask him?"

Chudd smiled. "You have a point there, and in due course I shall, but I'd like to hear your version first."

Billing looked at him in surprise. "You're making it pretty obvious, aren't you! Since when have I shopped a mate to assist the police!"

"I guessed that was what bothered you," Chudd remarked equably. "But you're wrong. I don't want you to shop him. I want you to help him." He waved a silencing hand as Billing was about to interrupt. "Just listen until I've finished. Sherbrook has confessed to a certain crime and at the moment I don't know whether it's true or false. If he's innocent, you could help to clear him."

"What crime?"

"That doesn't matter for the moment. Now then; did he ever tell you of any recent crime he'd committed?"

Billing ran his tongue round his mouth. "You say he's confessed to something?"

"Yes."

"And you want me to confirm or deny what he's told you?"

"I want to know whether he made a similar confession to you," Chudd replied patiently.

"How can I tell if I don't know what he's said to you?"

"Look . . . what's your name? Terence?"

"Terry."

"Well, look, Terry, let's have the position clear. Sherbrook has confessed to a crime. He's done so of his own free will, so he obviously won't mind if you repeat anything he told you to the same effect. On the other hand if he didn't tell you anything about it, that may go to show that it's a false confession and you will have helped to prevent an injustice. Now do you understand?"

Billing nodded slowly. "He did say something about a burglary job he'd done a few days before I met him."

"Did he say where."

"Is there somewhere called Elwick Common? It was some such name as that."

Chudd and Sergeant Roberts exchanged a rapid glance. "Did he tell you any details of the burglary?"

"Just said it was some old girl's house."

"What did he tell you about the old girl?"

"Nothing else."

"Did he say what had happened to her?"

Billing shook his head. "Can't remember that."

"Do you read the newspapers?"

"Look at one occasionally."

"Have you read anything about Elwick Common in the papers recently?"

"No. Don't read those bits anyway."

"What bits do you read?"

"The Strips and have a look at the pictures. That's about all."

"An old lady was murdered in Elwick Common a week ago," Chudd said. "Are you sure Sherbrook didn't tell you something about it?"

"No, he never actually mentioned a murder," Billing replied uneasily.

"What did he mention?"

"He did say this old girl whose house he was in caught him and he'd had to smack her one."

"He must have told you what happened after that."

"No, he didn't actually say."

"Even if he didn't actually say, what impression did you get?"

"That he might have hurt her quite badly." Billing shook his head slowly from side to side. "But he's a nut case that boy. You don't want to listen too much to what he says."

"In what way is he a nut case?"

"Just is. You've only got to talk to him."

"Where were you when he told you this?"

"In a cafe."

"The one in Elstree?"

"No, another."

"I'd like you to tell me what your movements were after you met Sherbrook in the first cafe."

98

"Later that day, we got a ride to Luton. And we stopped the night there."

"Where?"

"In a shed."

"And the next day?"

"We walked around a bit and then we got a ride to Bedford."

"And it was that evening, you were arrested?"

"S'right."

"So you were in Sherbrook's company for about a day and a half before you were picked up on the present charge?"

"That's it."

"What else did he tell you about his recent movements while you were together?"

"He never stopped talking but I didn't listen half the time."

"But what can you remember his saying about where he'd come from and what he'd been doing?" Chudd repeated patiently.

Billing shrugged to indicate growing boredom with so many questions. "Think he said he'd been living with an uncle at Chatham, but they didn't get on so he decided to quit. That was about a week before we met, and he'd just been drifting around."

"Doing housebreaking jobs?"

"You'd better ask him."

"But did he tell you?"

"Well you have to live somehow, don't you? And if you don't have any money, there's not much choice."

"There's such a thing as honest work," Sergeant Roberts broke in.

Billing glanced at him with one eyebrow quizzically raised. "That's O.K. for those who want it." His tone held a note of contempt as he added, "I'm not against it – for some."

"That sort of remark's not going to help you," Mr. Walls said sharply.

Billing appeared to be going to make a further retort but to have second thoughts on this. At all events he fell into silence.

Chudd said, "I don't think there's anything else I want to

ask you now, Terry, but it's more than likely I'll want to see you again."

"At least you know where to find me," Billing replied with a grin.

Even the Assistant Governor permitted himself a smile. "Cheeky young so-and-so," he remarked, after Billing had been escorted back to his cell. Five minutes later his place in the Governor's office had been taken by Sherbrook, a pasty-faced young man with close-set eyes and a head of overlong greasy-looking hair.

After the introductions had been made which nobody could fail to notice caused him a flush of satisfaction, Chudd said, "Will you repeat what you said to Mr. Hurley after exercise this afternoon."

"About killing the old girl?"

"Did you kill her?"

"Yeah, I killed her. Strangled her and stuffed her body beneath the bed." There was something harsh about his tone which made the words sound even more callous than seemed possible.

Chudd was shocked to realise suddenly that he hadn't yet cautioned Sherbrook and hastily made good this omission.

"That's O.K.," Sherbrook said airily. "I know you have to go through that bit of jazz, but I'm quite prepared to talk."

"Why did you kill her?"

" 'Cause she began to holler when she found me in her bedroom."

"In which room did you actually kill her?"

"In the bedroom like I'm telling you."

"Did you know her name?"

Sherbrook shook his head. "Still don't."

"How did you come to pick her house?"

"Just did. No particular reason."

"What were you doing in that road?"

"Scouting around."

"Do you mean looking for a house to burgle?"

"If you like."

"How did you get in?"

"I found the door open."

"Which door?"

"The front door."

"Sure about that?"

" 'Course I'm sure."

"What colour was the front door?"

"Didn't notice." Then as an apparent afterthought, "It was dark."

"What time *was* it?"

"About ten o'clock perhaps."

"You don't seem very sure."

"I don't have a watch."

"Wasn't there a clock in the house?"

"I didn't go in to look at the time."

"But you still might have noticed whether there was a clock."

"I didn't." His tone was petulant.

"What did you notice about the inside of the house?"

"I don't understand."

"You say you went into the bedroom?"

"Yes."

"Is that on the right or left when you reach the top of the stairs?"

"Right?"

"I'm asking you."

"Could have been left. One house is much like another and I've been inside a fair number just lately. Gets kind of confusing."

"I'm sure. Tell me something you can remember about this house."

"Nothing particular."

"But you must be able to."

"I've explained."

"But you don't leave bodies under beds in every house you visit," Chudd said sharply.

"I still don't remember anything special."

"You don't seem able to remember anything at all."

"I can remember killing her all right."

"How did you kill her?"

"Strangled her with a silk scarf."

"Did you take anything afterwards?"

"Bit of money."

"How much?"

"About six or seven quid. That's all there was." His tone sounded aggrieved.

"Where was it?"

"In a drawer in the bedroom."

"Loose or in a purse?"

"In a handbag."

"How long were you in the house?"

"Half an hour perhaps."

"Did you notice a table in the hall?"

"I think so."

"Did you notice anything on it?"

Sherbrook blinked uncertainly. "No."

"Sure there was nothing on it?"

"Could have been. Didn't notice things like that."

"By which door did you leave the house?"

"The front door."

"Did you leave it open behind you?"

"No, I closed it."

"And locked it?"

"Yes."

"What with?"

"I mean I let down the catch."

"And where did you go afterwards?"

"I got out of Elwick Common as fast as I could. A lorry-driver gave me a lift."

"Where to?"

"Near where the M.1 begins."

"Describe this lorry-driver."

"He was about thirty and had brown hair."

"What sort of accent?"

"Don't ask me! He just talked ordinary."

"Where'd he come from?"

"Near Birmingham he said."

"And whereabouts did he pick you up?"

"In Elwick Common."

"But where is Elwick Common?"

Once more Sherbrook's manner became hesitant. "On the outskirts."

"Is that all you can remember? Describe the exact point where this lorry picked you up? Were there fields around, were there houses or shops; was there a public house, a school in the vicinity? You must have noticed something."

"There were houses and shops," he said sullenly.

"Describe some of the shops?"

"I can't."

"Not even one of them?"

"They were just shops."

Chudd ran a finger across his upper lip, studied it thoughtfully for a second and said, "What decided you to make this confession?"

"Just did, that's all."

"Why didn't you go to the police immediately after you'd murdered Mrs. Hibbert and confess then?"

"Didn't want to."

"So I gather, but what I don't understand is your apparent change of heart."

Sherbrook squirmed a while and said defensively, "I'd been thinking about it and it was in my mind when Mr. Hurley sneered at me. It just kind of came out."

This at least Chudd regarded as feasible. There is nothing more frustrating to the criminal with exhibitionist tendencies than to remain in the shadows while his crime attracts all the limelight. Chudd could think of numerous cases where eventually a criminal's perverted sense of vanity had compelled him to step forward and hold up his hand so that public opinion could acknowledge his skill and bestow its dubious accolade. He could also recall one case which in a man serving a long sentence for robbery had confessed to an earlier murder simply to break the monotony of his daily life. It not only had this immediate effect but led not many weeks later to his being convicted, sentenced to death and executed. The irony of this situation had impressed Chudd deeply, since without the man's confession the crime would have remained unsolved for all time.

"Have you told Billing about the murder?" Chudd asked.

Again the cagey look came over Sherbrook's face. "Bits."

"Which bits?"

"Haven't told him all the details. Just mentioned I'd had to kill an old girl who squawked when she found me in her house."

"Where did you meet Billing for the first time?"

"In a cafe at Elstree."

"When?"

"Couple of days before we were picked up."

"Sure you weren't in Elwick Common together?"

"I was never in Elwick Common with Terry."

"Are you ready to make a statement in writing under caution, repeating all you've told me?"

"Sure, if that's what you want."

"It's not a question of what *I* want. It's up to you."

"Yeah, I'll make a statement."

"You can either write it yourself or, if you wish, Sergeant Roberts here will take down what you say."

"He can write it. I'm no scholar."

"And you realise that you may be charged with murder on what you say?"

"They can't hang you these days, can they?"

"No."

"I'm ready to start when you are." His tone was cocky. He might have been a film star giving an autograph to an importunate fan.

"Just one final thing," Chudd said. "If by any chance this confession is proved to be false you'll be up to your neck in trouble for causing a public mischief."

"What's that lot mean?"

"It's a criminal offence to waste the time of the police to the detriment of the public at large. That's it in a nutshell."

Sherbrook gave a shrug, as if to indicate unconcern with such technical trifles.

After he had been taken to another room to make his statement, Mr. Walls said to Chudd, "Do you believe him?"

Chudd was silent for a time. "I don't know."

"Perhaps that wasn't the right question. Are you going to charge him?"

"Not immediately. Somebody else can decide that. Probably the D.P.P."

"How can you not charge him if he makes a confession which could be true?"

"I agree, that's the difficulty. But did you notice the way he became all vague when I tried to tie him down to detail. And that business about not noticing the time when he was in the house, why the place is alive with clocks. They line the walls and jump at you round every corner."

Mr. Walls pursed his lips. "Lads like Sherbrook are not particularly observant. They don't possess the same inquiring mind of better educated boys."

"You don't need an inquiring mind to notice the clocks in Mrs. Hibbert's house. Even a blind moron could hardly fail to observe that the house was stuffed with clocks."

"Apart from his vagueness about details, do you have any other reason for doubting his story?"

"Let me put it this way. I wish I found it more convincing than I do."

"Doesn't it fit in with what you've found?"

"It's not that. It's just that it has the wrong feel."

"You mean, you hadn't previously thought of this as the sort of murder committed by a Sherbrook type youth?"

Chudd smiled wryly. "As a matter of fact, a D.I. on the case has thought all along that it bore the marks of a Borstal boy murder."

"There you are then!"

"If only there weren't others with apparent motives and opportunities." Chudd remarked gloomily. "The whole case is one mass of unexplained ends."

"Well, it seems to me your troubles are over," Mr. Walls said briskly. "With a signed confession in your pocket you're home and dry."

Chudd rose. "Is it possible to ensure that Sherbrook and Billing don't communicate with each other? I'd like them kept well apart for the time being."

"It won't be easy, but I'll try. It'll mean detailing an officer to keep them under constant observation whenever they're out of their cells. And you realise, they'll be going off to court together next week. There's nothing I can do about that."

"I'll have a word with the local police. I want to see the officer in charge of their case in any event. Meanwhile, I'll keep in touch with you."

"And I'll see that nothing leaks from here. I don't imagine you want this latest development noised around."

"Too true I don't."

"As you're probably aware the prison grapevine is quite the most sensitive and alert of any. However, I'll do my best."

Two and a half hours had passed since Chudd and Sergeant Roberts had arrived at the prison, and it was shortly after ten o'clock when they left and made their way to the local police station. There, by lucky chance, they found Detective Constable White who was the officer in charge of the case against Sherbrook and Billing.

"I'm on nights all this week," White remarked. "That's how I came to be lumbered with this pair of monkeys." He let out a low whistle of interest when Chudd explained the purpose of their visit.

"Of course, I didn't actually arrest them. That was Police Constable Parry. I expect you'd like to have a word with him, too?"

"If he's around."

"I saw him when I came in an hour ago. I'll fetch him."

"Before you do that, there are a few things I'd like to ask

you. First, were you present when these two were searched?"

"As a matter of fact I searched Billing and P.C. Parry searched the other."

"What was found on them?"

"I can easily tell you that if you'll just hold on while I get the charge sheets. I retrieved them from the court after the remand as the charge hadn't been properly worded and the clerk said it ought to be amended."

"Perhaps you'd also let the senior C.I.D. officer on duty know I'm here."

D.C. White dived out of the room to return two minutes later waving the charge sheets as if they were maps of buried treasure.

"The acting Detective Superintendent will be over in about twenty minutes."

"Don't tell him I asked, but what's his name?"

"Smith."

"Yes, of course," Chudd said blandly. White handed him the charge sheets and he studied them in silence for a minute. "Nothing here to help me."

"Were you looking for something in particular, sir?"

"Yes, a key."

"Don't remember seeing any keys. Anyway, it'd be on the sheet, if one had been found."

Chudd glanced once more at the list of prisoner's property recorded on each charge sheet, bearing at the bottom the signature of the owner.

"Just over four pounds on Billing and eighteen shillings on Sherbrook," he murmured. "Otherwise just the usual bits and pieces. Cigarette lighter, ballpoint pen, pocket diary." He looked up, "Anything of interest in the diary found on Sherbrook?"

"It's unused. Imagine he picked it up somewhere because he liked the feel or colour of it, not for recording his social life."

Chudd handed the charge sheets back to D.C. White. "Pity about the key. That really would have proved something. I take it that Sherbrook never showed any inclination to make any confessions to you about the murder?"

"Not a thing. They were both pretty quiet and resigned when I saw them. Didn't seem they wanted to talk about anything."

"Did either of them make a statement admitting the present offence?"

"No. They were caught red-handed so I didn't care whether they did or not. Incidentally, P.C. Parry is downstairs if you'd like to have a word with him."

"Please."

But Parry was unable to shed any helpful light on Chudd's problem. He told how he'd been patrolling beside a factory wall, when he'd heard suspicious sounds coming from a yard round which the administrative offices were situated. He had climbed to the top of the wall and, on looking over, seen Sherbrook and Billing trying a door which was marked "Cashier". He had jumped down and told them they were under arrest and they had apparently accompanied him to the police station as quiet as lambs.

He had just finished reciting his evidence to Chudd when the door opened and the acting Detective Superintendent came in.

"I'd have been here if I'd known you were coming," he said, as he shook hands.

"It's for me to apologise," Chudd replied quickly, mindful of the state of congealed unhelpfulness into which police relations can sometimes fall through breaches of protocol. "But the fact is we left Elwick Common at a couple of minutes notice and, anyway, didn't know until after our visit to the prison that we'd have the further call to make."

"That's O.K.," Smith said. "What else can we do for you?"

"I'm not sure for the moment. Will there be any difficulty about obtaining a further remand when they come up next Wednesday? It mayn't even be necessary, but it might help if I haven't been able to get instructions about charging Sherbrook before then."

"No, that can easily be fixed. The Clerk to the Justices is an accommodating fellow and it'll require only a quiet word of explanation to him. And neither of them are legally represented at present so there can't be any trouble from that quarter."

"That's fine then," Chudd said. "I'll get a decision as quickly as I can but with the weekend intervening, it's bound to be Tuesday at the earliest before I hear anything."

"Despite having his signed written confession in your pocket, you weren't prepared to charge him straightaway?"

Not for the first time that evening Chudd wondered if he was being over cautious. He was pretty certain that Inspector Bracker wouldn't have left the prison without charging Sherbrook, and it seemed that Superintendent Smith wouldn't have hesitated. Had years at the Yard sapped his initiative, turned him into a bureaucrat? He trusted not, he didn't really think so, though he realised that others might. Viewing the facts as dispassionately as he could, it seemed there was every reason for not rushing in and charging Sherbrook without further inquiry. If he had been at large, the decision would have been a great deal more awkward, since a failure to charge him might result in his disappearance. But this was the beauty of the present situation, Sherbrook was lodged securely in prison – or as securely as any prisoner is these days – and so a decision didn't have to be taken on the spur of the moment. No, the more he reflected, the more certain he felt that he had decided aright. The only possible reason for having charged him immediately would have been for public effect, for satisfying the personal urge for immediate action. But it so happened this was not one of his urges. That's why he had never fancied himself as a Flying Squad Officer. Their job demanded the making of such decisions as a sort of reflex. There was seldom time to weigh up pros and cons and strike a considered balance. He returned his mind to Superintendent Smith's question.

"Nothing's going to be lost by holding off for a few days. The case isn't as straightforward as it may seem and I'm not convinced that Sherbrook's confession is the whole truth."

"He only has himself to blame if he is charged."

"True enough, but since time is on our side on this particular issue, I'd rather pause now than charge down the wrong path and have to retrace my steps later."

On the way back to London in the car, Chudd turned to Sergeant Roberts and said, "Would you have charged him?"

"I would have, sir, On the other hand I don't think anyone can say you were wrong not to do so in the circumstances." With a grin he went on, "I'm pretty sure we do shoot off the mark too quickly sometimes, but that's the sort of job ours is. You don't have time to think everything out and so you just grab at the fellow for fear he'll vanish if you don't."

It was one o'clock on Saturday morning when Chudd let himself quietly into his home. For most people, the weekend had begun eight hours before. He reckoned he'd be doing well if he managed to take three hours off on Sunday afternoon.

On this occasion, sounds indicated that every member of his family was asleep. Anyone was crazy who thought you could be a husband and a father as well as a police officer, he reflected wearily as he began to undress in the dark.

Then suddenly he brightened. He had, at least, gone through a whole day without mislaying his pipe.

8

AT breakfast the next morning, Kate said, "You won't be working the whole weekend, will you?"

"I hope not," he said with a resigned smile.

"No seriously, Peter, I insist you devote some time to your family and unless I tie you down now, I know what's going to happen. You'll spend all to-day and Sunday at the station like a dog waiting for its master, and I shall have three fractious boys on my hands. Well, two anyway."

"Not to mention an ill-used gremlin on your shoulder to contend with," he added.

"Oh, I'm used to him," she replied in a tone which made him realise that his normally unruffled wife really was put out this time. "I dare say work has to come first, but that doesn't mean to say it has to fill second, third and hundredth places as well in your life. It's time the police realised that its officers' children will grow up into delinquents if it deprives them of their fathers seven days a week."

"I promise that we'll all go out somewhere tomorrow afternoon," he said emphatically. "I shall probably have to look in at the station in the morning, but I'll take the afternoon off even if I have to work all night afterwards."

"I'm delighted to hear it," Kate said. "Even if that isn't the dutiful answer."

They both laughed and the tension dissolved. "I suppose every family goes through these rough patches," she went on, "but this one is our roughest to date."

"I know. The move, David not settling down, Superintendent Manton away, this murder. It certainly has been a rugged time for all of us. I agree about police hours. It's damnable, but what's the solution?"

"I don't think it would be so bad for the wives if they didn't always have the feeling that their husbands secretly relished working eighty hours a week; that they didn't really envy the five-day week boys however much they might protest to the contrary."

"Hmm, I wonder. . . ."

"I'm sure of it."

"It's true you have to be dedicated to the job if you're going to survive."

"It's like being the dedicated victims of rapacious giant."

"I could retire, I suppose, and find another job which would give me more time with you and the boys. Perhaps we ought to consider it."

Kate looked at him aghast. "Darling, I never meant you to take me all that seriously. Let's face it, I'm a dedicated police officer's wife, even if I do occasionally sound a blast of insurrection. And I've no wish to become anything else so long as you're doing what makes you happiest and provided I continue to remain sound in mind and limb."

"You're the family linch-pin, Kate" he said affectionately. "Without you, we'd be in five separate orbits." He paused. "Incidentally, where are the boys?"

"Timmy's gone off to the park to collect some special leaves for his caterpillar. Andrew's reading a comic stretched out on his bed which he's meant to be making and David is still asleep. I told him he could lie in this morning as he was late last night."

"What was he doing?"

"There was a special film show at the school for the cricketers. It was only arranged at the last minute, that's why you didn't know about it." She leaned across the table and poured him another cup of tea. "Where'll we go on Sunday?"

"Do we have any choice? Doesn't it have to be polo?"

"I suppose it does."

"There's always one member of the family in need of a bit of salvaging, and it happens to be David at the moment." He caught her eye. "All right, you don't have to say it! But I'll be salvaged just by being out with you all."

"Careful, you're becoming sentimental. . . . So polo it'll be. We must expect some protests from Andrew and Timmy. They'd already made up their minds they were going to have their own respective ways."

"They'll probably enjoy watching polo when it comes to the point. When I was their age I used to revel at bicycle polo until I broke three windows in the course of one afternoon and lost several spokes from my front wheel which brought the season to an abrupt end."

"I hope you won't encourage bicycle polo on our back lawn," Kate remarked, gazing over the small patch of rough turf. "In the six weeks we've lived here, it's been ravaged by cricket, football, archery and some assorted circus turns."

112

Chudd grinned. "Poor kids, being brought up in a town." He glanced at the electric clock on the kitchen wall and rose. "I'll try and be home at a reasonable hour this evening."

"What time could that be?"

"About five or six."

"If that's definite, I'll kill the fatted calf."

"Kill away. I'll be there." He went round to where Kate was sitting and kissed her. "I didn't lose my pipe yesterday," he added in a pleased tone, pulling it from his jacket pocket and gazing at it with slight wonderment.

"Off to work with you, Maigret," Kate said, giving him a gentle push toward the door.

On arrival at his office, he 'phoned the Yard to see if the Deputy Commander was expected in that morning. He wasn't, but Chudd was given his home telephone number and advised he could call him there without fear of ructions.

"Who wants him?" a female voice enquired when Chudd got through. He then heard the voice repeat at a muffled distance, "It's a Chief Inspector someone wants to speak to you. Richard."

It sounded funny hearing the Deputy Commander addressed as Richard. There was no reason why he shouldn't have the name, but Chudd had never thought of him as other than the Deputy Commander, Mr. Ellis, or old beanpole, and Richard didn't seem to share a place with any of those. His thoughts were interrupted by the sound of the receiver at the other end being scraped against a hard surface and a second later he heard the Deputy Commander's voice.

"Who's there?"

"Chudd, sir. I apologise for calling you at home."

"That's all right. I was fitting a new washer on a tap and had just received a doucheful of water in the face. Glad to have an excuse to do something else."

Without further invitation, Chudd related the events of the previous evening and concluded, "The point is do we charge Sherbrook, sir?"

"You obviously don't think we should?"

"How can we not?"

"The answer to that one is, we oughtn't to charge him unless we accept his confession as true."

"It could be true. On the other hand, most of the details he gave have appeared in the press."

"But not all?"

"I can't cite any particular item he told us which hasn't because I haven't read every report which has appeared, but there could be some that haven't."

"Isn't it important to find out?"

"Ye-es,"

"Why the hesitation?"

"I don't really believe he did the murder, sir."

"Why not?"

"Because I don't believe all the business of the deceased being about to change her will, and telling lies about her cousin in Canada arriving any day, and getting rid of Peggy Dunkley are so many red herrings, which they must be if the murder was committed by a youth like Sherbrook just happening to wander across the scene at that juncture. It doesn't make sense."

"Murders often don't," the Deputy Commander broke in. "Because human conduct frequently doesn't. I shouldn't let that bother you over-much. As I see it, the important thing is to find out how far you can corroborate Sherbrook's confession by independent evidence. If you can do that; i.e., prove that Sherbrook has admitted to things which only the murderer can have known, then obviously, there's no alternative to charging him. Anyway, who'll want an alternative? We'll have done our job and solved the ruddy case and you can throw all your red herrings back in the ocean."

"If they are red herrings. . . . "

The Deputy Commander made a "tch" sound and said, "All right, let's have them enumerated. You'd better get them off your chest. Now then, what are your reasons, one, two, three, for not wishing to accept Sherbrook's confession, apart from its apparent vagueness on certain matters of detail?"

114

"They all boil down to one thing, sir. I don't believe that this was the crime of a casual intruder. I was prepared to think so at the beginning, but not now."

"Reasons, one, two, three," the Deputy Commander broke in impatiently.

Chudd took a deep breath and quickly tried to marshal his thoughts into a semblance of order. He was being called upon to justify in logical argument, what instinct and a series of disconnected facts led him to believe.

"First there's the whole mysterious business of Peggy Dunkley's departure. If she's not telling the truth, then the odds must be that she committed the murder. And if she is telling the truth, it's obvious that Mrs. Hibbert had something to hide. Why did she want to get rid of Dunkley? Why did she give a false reason for doing so? And then there's the highly significant fact that she was about to change her will – or rather, that's the not unreasonable inference." He paused and reflected on what he had just said. "In some way, sir, those events must be connected. They all form part of an, as yet, jumbled pattern. A pattern into which Sherbrook's intervention doesn't fit."

"And what about your clock-winder chap, how does he fit?"

"He doesn't," Chudd admitted, unhappily. The silence which now ensued at the other end of the line, however, encouraged him to think that his argument had at least made some impression on the Deputy Commander.

At length Mr. Ellis said, "Thank heaven Sherbrook is shut up in gaol. It does give us a bit of time to think. We'll have a word on Monday and possibly go and see the D.P.P. Though frankly I suspect the problem whether or not to charge is ours, not the lawyers'. If we accept his confession, we must charge him. If we don't, and we have sound reasons for disbelieving him, equally obviously we shouldn't charge him. It's as simple as that – if you call that simple. In the meantime you'd better go through that statement of his with a toothcomb and be ready to indicate on Monday which bits, if any, clearly implicate him as the person who must have committed the murder."

"Certainly I'll do that, sir," Chudd replied, though without enthusiasm. It was already his view that there were no such bits. Thinking back now he realised that Sherbrook had given him the impression of someone who had attempted to learn something by heart and who had recapitulated it not very accurately. There came suddenly into his mind a picture of himself thirty years ago standing up in class and taking a deep breath before launching at breakneck speed into Milton's *Paradise Lost*. By about the sixth line, however, he had invariably resorted to Peter Chudd's own improvised version of the poem and a couple of lines later he would run out of steam altogether. There would be a painful silence before the English master, who had a deep voice and was the colour of French mustard, would say, "Not only is paradise lost but Chudd as well. Perhaps he will be able to make good his outrage to Milton by spending Saturday afternoon writing the poem out. It'll be much better for him than playing football." He would fix Chudd with a glinting eye. "I'll expect you here at two o'clock, Chudd, and let us hope that paradise can be regained before nightfall."

It was hardly surprising that he had grown up to identify the English poets with this particular master and to regard the lot as scourges whose weals still showed upon his hide.

The recollection was so vivid that the Deputy Commander's voice seemed an unwarranted intrusion.

"Try and take a bit of time off over the weekend. You don't want to run yourself into the ground."

"I was proposing to take the family out tomorrow afternoon sir."

"Sound idea. How's your wife liking Elwick Common?"

"Settling down well, sir."

"And the boys?"

"The eldest's taking a bit of time, the other two are fine."

Chudd heard a muffled shout, followed by Mr. Ellis saying urgently, "I must dash. That tap's just blown up and drenched my wife."

Chudd sat back in his chair and contemplated the further

wall of his office. There seemed very little he could positively
achieve between now and Monday morning, and yet it never
seriously entered his head to walk out of the station and spend
the weekend as other people were doing. Perhaps Kate did
have a point when she suggested they were the willing, eager
slaves of the service to which they had dedicated themselves.
His glance fell on the slab of paper in his in-tray. Anyway, even
if there was little he could do in connection with the murder
enquiry, there was certainly enough other matter to occupy his
attention the whole weekend. Those wretched number one
dockets for a start, though he'd almost prefer to copy out
Paradise Lost than embark on those. They were even an encour-
agement to spin out the murder enquiry. But eventually he
would have to bring himself to pursue them through to their
invariably arid conclusion. Heaven, what a fearful waste of
time most of them were! They were profoundly depressing to
Chudd and the great majority of his colleagues who liked to
regard themselves not only as members of a proud service but
as ordinary men with normal instincts of decency and fair-
mindedness.

He roused himself out of his gloomy reverie and pushed
the pile of number ones further from him. Then lifting the
receiver, he put through another call to the Yard, this time to
the laboratory to discover how far they'd got in their examination of the articles he'd submitted. Even before the connection
was made he knew it would be like rubbing a sore and that the
answer was likely to be unsatisfactory. And so it turned out.

"Afraid we haven't been able to complete your job yet,"
one of the liaison officers told him.

"Have you even begun?" he asked, a trifle testily.

"Now look, sir, it's not our fault if we're understaffed and
overworked. We do our best, but jobs have to take their turn."

Chudd wished he'd never made the call. He didn't want to
pick a quarrel, though this seemed inevitable if their conversation continued. Anyway, he was in their hands and dependent
on the lab's good-will, so he could only back down.

"Yes, I know," he said wearily.

"Any particular help you were hoping to get from us in this case?" the liaison officer enquired, rather in the tone of a shop assistant who has successfully beaten off a complaining customer.

"I can't say there was."

"Pity. It makes it easier when the officer in charge of the case can give us an indication or two."

"Well, do your best for me."

"We always do our best for everyone, sir."

Chudd could have kicked his backside. Who'd the fellow think he was with that smug line of talk! He now quite definitely regretted having made the enquiry. It was an ill-considered action which he should have foreseen would end unsatisfactorily. Well, he had foreseen it, but his hopes had outweighed his judgment. What he hadn't foreseen was that he would be put in his place with such bland impudence.

The truth was, as he'd known all along, that the lab. were not likely to be able to assist him until an arrest had been made and some control samples were available for comparative purposes. And it didn't look as though they'd be able to help him very much even then. There were no bloodstains anywhere and the only possibility was that some foreign matter might be found adhering to the articles submitted which could later be tied up with something from a suspect. But what? A hair perhaps. Supposing an unidentified hair was to be found amongst Mrs. Hibbert's clothing, he'd have to obtain samples from Sherbrook and Peggy Dunkley and Stack. Supposing . . . He'd a good mind to ring the lab again and tell that liaison officer to pull his finger out and search for hairs which weren't the deceased's.

For the rest of the morning he read, re-read and then again read through Sherbrook's statement, though without any flash of inspiration. He realised that if he wanted to believe Sherbrook guilty, the statement afforded support for such a view, but since this wasn't his belief, it failed to convince him. It was that sort of statement, you could read into it what you wanted to believe. But what right had he not to accept it as the truth? He wasn't judge or jury, so why assume their function? Anyway, he'd passed the problem to others and would be quite prepared to abide by their decision.

He looked at his watch and wondered whether Detective Sergeant Roberts was in the building and would like to slip out for a beer with him.

Every Saturday at one o'clock when Mr. Mundy closed the shop for an hour, Arthur Stack would hurry off to The Rising Sun to meet his pal, George, and indulge in a little midday drinking. Just a couple of pints, and certainly never more than three as too much beer didn't go well with finicking about with the delicate innards of watches.

On this particular Saturday George was, as usual, there first and sitting in his customary corner of the public bar.

"Hello, Arthur," he called out as Stack entered. "Come and sit down. It's my turn to get the first pint to-day."

Stack accepted the tankard with muttered thanks and took a deep draught, sucking in his lips to relish the after-flavour.

"How've things been with you this week, Arthur?" George enquired, as he always did. The surprising feature being that he listened to the answer as well.

"Been feeling a bit under the weather as a matter of fact."

"There's a germ going about," George said comfortingly. "You've probably caught it. Several of my mates at work have been quite bad. Had a headache?"

"A bit."

"And tummy pains?"

"Pains all over."

George nodded in a knowing fashion. "That's it. You've got the bug. You'll probably run a bit of a temperature, too, toward the end. If you take my advice, you'll spend tomorrow in bed." He peered into Stack's face. "You look a mite off colour."

During their second pint, George maintained a flow of comment on his own week's activities. When he returned from the bar with their third pints, he said, "The police don't seem to be getting anywhere with the murder of that old woman you knew, Arthur." To his surprise, Arthur's hand began to tremble unaccountably so that some of his beer was spilled and he was forced to put down his tankard on the table. "Not feeling too good, Arthur?" he asked anxiously.

"No, I'm all right."

"You've gone a shocking colour all of a sudden."

"It was your mentioning Mrs. Hibbert like that. I thought a lot of her, you see."

George nodded understandingly. "Have the police seen you over it?"

"Yes."

"Not that I imagine you were able to help them very much."

"No."

"Come to think of it, I remember your looking a bit shaken when I saw you last Saturday morning. That was the day she was meant to have been killed, wasn't it?"

Stack drained his tankard and stared morosely into its depths for a full minute before replying.

"I'm up to my neck in trouble, George," he suddenly blurted out. "I don't know what to do."

"You'd better tell me, Arthur. Perhaps I'll be able to help."

"I doubt it, but I'll be glad to tell you all the same. I must get it off my conscience or I'll go crazy. You see, I've lied to the police. I told them the old lady was alive when I called there last Saturday morning and that I spoke to her. But she wasn't, she was dead. But I swear I never killed her."

"A Mr. Stack and a Mr. Farthing want to see you, sir," Cadet Temple announced on the line. "They say it's very urgent. Or rather Mr. Farthing does. The other one hasn't said a word. He looks like a ghost."

"Have them sent up," Chudd replied, and quickly put out of sight in a drawer the ham sandwich he'd been eating when the 'phone rang.

George Farthing came into the room with the affability of a small town mayor.

"My name's Farthing and I believe you know my friend, Mr. Stack. He has some important information to give you about the murder of Mrs. Hibbert and I said I'd come along with him to provide moral support. That's right, isn't it. Arthur?"

Stack nodded uneasily and George Farthing went on, "Well, are you going to tell our friend here or do you want me to?"

"You."

"Mind if we sit down?" he enquired.

"Go ahead," Chudd said, wondering what would follow next.

"It's quite simple. We've just come round to correct a misstatement of fact Mr. Stack made to you. I understand he told you that Mrs. Hibbert was alive when he called last Saturday. It turns out she wasn't. She was already dead and he thought you ought to know."

"Is that true?" Chudd asked sharply, looking at Stack.

"Yes. She was definitely dead. I'm afraid I wasn't exactly truthful."

"I think," Chudd said, "that you had better tell me the story yourself from the beginning."

"Go on, Arthur," George urged, "you tell him just like you told me. If you tell the truth, you haven't got anything to worry about."

Chudd hesitated whether to correct this dubious sentiment, especially when expressed within the walls of a police station, but decided to let it go. In due course he might feel obliged to caution Stack, but until that moment arrived it was obviously in the police interest to say nothing which might shake his already infirm resolution.

"I was nervous when you called at the shop on Tuesday," Stack said in a tone of faint aggression. "You took me by surprise coming there like that and wanting to see me. You ought to have given me some warning and then I could have met you and Mr. Mundy wouldn't have known."

"Get on with it, Arthur," George broke in amiably.

"I will, but I want him to understand that it was because I was flustered I didn't tell the exact truth before."

121

As he listened patiently to this preamble, Chudd recognised all the signs of someone whose conscience was squirming like an impaled worm. The equivocations which converted down-right lies into such euphemisms as "misstatements" and "not the exact truth". He could see that this was not going to be a session of frank soul-baring, but of the truth emerging shyly and hesitantly when it thought no one was looking.

Chudd decided to provide a helping hand. "First of all is it correct that you arrived at Mrs. Hibbert's around eleven o'clock last Saturday morning?"

"Yes, that's the complete truth."

"And let yourself in by the side door which was unlocked?"

Stack nodded eagerly. "That's the truth, too."

"Carry on from there."

Stack let out a small groan of anguish. "I began to wind the downstairs clocks. I thought it funny there was no sign of Mrs. Hibbert. She'd usually call out, 'Is that you, Arthur?' as soon as she heard me come in. But I just assumed she must be upstairs in the . . . the bathroom, so I carried on. When I'd finished below, I went up. Her bedroom door was half-open and I looked through the crack but I couldn't see her inside, so I just knocked and then entered." Stack swallowed nerv-ously. "Well, I'd just wound the clock in her bedroom and was looking around thinking it was funny her being out and leaving me no message like. On the few occasions she was out when I called, she'd always leave a note on the kitchen table, you see. Anyway, there I was, standing there a bit puzzled when I sort of noticed one side of the counterpane on the bed was hitched up and I saw a hand underneath the bed. Then I bent down and took a proper look and realised it was Mrs. Hibbert."

"Could you tell that she was dead?" Chudd broke in.

"I touched her hand and it was quite cold." He gave a violent shiver.

"What did you do then?"

"My first thought was to get away from the house as quickly as possible. But I realised it would look suspicious if I left some of the clocks unwound, so I finished them and then I left."

"Which way did you go out?"

"By the same door, except that I let the catch down and slammed it behind me."

A silence ensued during which George Farthing looked intently from one to the other like the neutral chairman of a television panel.

"And why," Chudd enquired in an apparently casual tone. "didn't you immediately report what you'd found to the police?"

He was now all ready to caution Stack depending on the answer he received.

"Because I was frightened."

"Frightened of what?"

"That you'd think I'd killed her." Before Chudd had time to comment, he went on, "I realise now how foolish I've been and that I've made matters much worse by not coming to the police in the first place, but I still swear I didn't murder her."

"Well?"

"That's all. Honest it is."

George Farthing shook his head in slow reproof. "You'll feel a lot better if you get everything off your chest, Arthur. Would you like me to tell him the rest?" Stack nodded in mute discomfort. Turning to Chudd, Farthing said, "It's like this and I'm sure you'll understand, but Arthur's had a bit of bad conscience for some time over his Saturday visits to Mrs. Hibbert's on account of nicking things. Nothing serious, mind you, but temptation was put in his way and I'm afraid he succumbed. Mr. Mundy doesn't pay him a decent wage and . . . well, Arthur's occasionally helped himself to bits of cash he's found lying around at Mrs. Hibbert's. He tells me, and I'm sure it's the truth, he's never taken more than a quid or so at one time and he's not had more than ten or twelve pounds in all. Silly of him, of course," Farthing added in a tone of paternal forgiveness, "but there can't be many of us who mightn't have fallen in the same circumstances. The Devil knows how to bait a trap for each of us."

Chudd looked across at Stack whose head was sunk on his

chest in a sculptor's pose of remorse. "Is this true?" he asked, and quickly proceeded to caution him.

"Yes."

"Did you take anything last Saturday?"

"No. Definitely not."

"I propose to ask you some questions, which you don't have to answer."

"All right, I'll answer them if I can."

George Farthing nodded approvingly.

"Have you anything fresh to say about Saturday's newspaper which we found on the hall table?"

"I put it there. It was still stuck in the letter-box when I arrived and I put it on the table."

"And did you notice an unposted airmail letter on the table?"

"Yes, to someone in Canada."

"And a key with a piece of red ribbon tied to it?"

Stack shook his head. "There was definitely no key on the table."

"Are you absolutely sure?"

"Positive. I'll swear an oath."

"You don't have to do that," Chudd said coolly, "but are you quite, quite certain?"

"As certain as I am that I'm sitting here in your office."

The presence of Saturday's newspaper folded neatly on the hall table was now explained, but Peggy Dunkley's missing door-key remained a mystery.

Chudd said slowly, "I'm still not sure that I understand why your thefts from Mrs. Hibbert made it necessary for you to behave as you did."

Stack looked uncomfortable. "I thought she'd begun to have her suspicions about me. I'd caught her looking at me a bit oddly once or twice, and on one occasion she came into her bedroom just as I was closing the drawer in which she kept her handbag. She didn't actually see what I was doing, but she gave me a funny look."

"And you thought she might have passed on her suspicions to someone?"

"Yes. So that I'd be an immediate suspect when you realised I'd been at the house on Saturday morning. I couldn't deny that because of the clocks being wound up. I reckoned the best line to take was that she'd been alive when I called. I didn't know when I said that that you'd been able to work out the actual time of death. The newspapers were misleading. The one I read said she'd been killed sometime between Friday night and early Sunday morning."

Chudd looked at him with an expression of disgust. It seemed likely that he had now told the truth, but his readiness to nurse a grievance against those who he obviously felt had let him down was nauseating. It was the fault of others that he'd been induced to lie, and now that his lies had been proved to have short legs he felt affronted.

"Nothing will happen to him, will it, over these other matters?" George Farthing asked.

"I can't say at this stage. I'll have to report it and he may be charged with larceny." Chudd felt like adding, "And as far as I'm concerned, I hope he is." He addressed himself once more to Stack. "Are you willing to make a written statement setting out all you've told me?"

"Yes, anything to help you."

"You won't be making it to help me and I must remind you of the caution. What about it?"

"I'd like to make a statement and clear the whole matter up. After that, shall I be allowed to go?"

"Certainly. You're not under arrest – yet."

When the statement had been completed and signed, Arthur Stack and George Farthing departed, leaving Chudd to reflect with satisfaction on the disposal of at least one loose end. Stack's insistence that Mrs. Hibbert was alive when everything else indicated the contrary had been inexplicable and frustrating. But now that this point had been resolved, he fell to contemplating the further implications. Of one thing he was now wholly convinced, namely that it was the murderer who had taken the door-key from the table – or who had never left it there in the first place.

Around four o'clock when he was making a brief search for his pipe – it had become hidden beneath a folder – he came across his half-eaten ham sandwich. He was about to begin munching it again when he remembered that Kate would be preparing something special for supper that evening and that he'd do better to let his appetite grow.

Even though there were people on duty, Elwick Common Police Station bore the somnolent air of a Saturday afternoon. This wouldn't last beyond early evening, however, when the first drunks began to be brought in. From about ten till eleven-thirty it would be really hectic as they arrived and, subject to their degree of intoxication, were charged and bailed, or put into the cells to sober up until this could be done. The noise from the cells on these occasions was tremendous, bangs and shouts blending with snores and singing to provide an authentic Hogarthian touch.

When Chudd entered the general office downstairs on his way out of the building, Police Cadet Temple was the only person immediately in sight. He was hunched in front of the station switchboard but looked round quickly when he heard footsteps.

"Got to go now, darling," Chudd heard him hiss as he whipped out a plug and swung round.

"Afternoon, sir," he said cheerfully. "How's the enquiry going?"

There was something disarming about his impudent breeziness which had several times saved him from scorching rebukes, though it was still a matter for speculation whether he'd ever survive long enough to become a useful police officer. Chudd hoped that he would. Inspector Bracker, on the other hand, prophesied an early and well-deserved boot up the backside for him.

"Slowly," Chudd replied.

"You haven't had many breaks, have you?"

"I'm not aware of having had any."

Cadet Temple chuckled. "Did you know it was I who took the call which started the whole thing off, sir?"

"No."

"Yes, when that old girl 'phoned to say she was worried about her neighbour."

"That certainly gives you a direct interest in the case," Chudd remarked.

Shortly afterwards the switchboard began to emit a subdued but insistent sound, and when Temple showed no inclination to answer it, Chudd felt obliged to cut in on his scathing condemnation of the English football selectors and point out that somebody might be wishing to report another murder. He then fled before Cadet Temple, who had as little respect for protocol as a torpedo, could involve him.

He had a small experiment he wished to try out on himself which meant a visit to Mrs. Hibbert's house. It was a pleasant sunny afternoon and time, for once, not snapping at his heels, he decided to walk. Gazing at the almost identical fronts of the houses he passed, he reflected on the anonymity of life in a suburb such as Elwick Common. Some suburbs acquired, or managed to maintain, a distinct character of their own, but Elwick Common could never have been other than amorphous. From being a small village ten miles from London's centre, it had grown, like a plain child into a desperately ordinary adult. Chudd couldn't believe that it had managed to charm at any stage of its development. It could only have expanded because people had to live somewhere. To him, it would never be more than another posting. But then he wasn't a townsman at heart, even though he had spent the last twenty odd years in the capital. He suddenly found himself passing the playing fields of the school where Peggy Dunkley taught. Four games of netball were going on, one of them clearly a school match as small knots of girls were dotted round the touchline and piping squeals of excitement floated across to him as he paused to watch, after spotting Peggy who was umpiring the match. She moved easily and athletically, blowing shrill blasts on her whistle and controlling the game with commanding gestures.

What an enigma she presented in the case, Chudd reflected. Apart from the fact he had no evidence and couldn't somehow bring himself to believe she had murdered Mrs. Hibbert, she had all the necessary attributes. Physically she was capable of murder and mentally, too, though that applies to everyone given the right set of circumstances. She had opportunity and she had one known, if insubstantial, motive. Why then didn't he think she'd committed the crime? He had his doubts about Sherbrook, too, and *he'd* made a confession. Instinct, intuition, call it what you will, was a valuable aid in the investigation of crime, but one had no right to off-set it against facts, and wasn't that just what he was doing! If he was forced to make a choice, Peggy Dunkley would be his candidate for murderer ahead of Sherbrook. That young man was no more than an unstable exhibitionist. He could only conclude that his reluctance to see Peggy as murderer was emotional. She had struck him as essentially decent even though she was not a person with whom he felt any particular bond of understanding. But that was absurd. A large number of people who committed murder were essentially decent. Certainly most of those with whom he'd been associated had managed without much difficulty to evoke his compassion. After all penologists and social reformers never tired of proclaiming that murder was a crime apart. There were, of course, the premeditated murders, the callous and brutal murders, the hopelessly mad murders, but put all these together and they still formed the exception. The great majority were committed by people who'd led blameless lives until a flashpoint was reached. The Heaths, the Haighs and the Christies were the exceptions. The Smiths and the Browns, unless they happened to have drowned brides or shot police-men, committed their murders and passed from view with the public largely unaware of their existence and wholly indifferent to their fate.

Chudd's thoughts were interrupted by an extra long blast on the whistle and the match was over. He turned away before Peggy Dunkley noticed him. Of one thing he was sure. If she had murdered Mrs. Hibbert, it was for a reason not yet un-covered. This brought him to the further reflection that the whole background of the case was far more opaque than he would choose to have it.

Ten minutes later he turned into Cresta Drive. He was just half way up the path to her front door when he was hailed from the bushes on his right.

"Good afternoon, Inspector Chudd." He recognised Miss Frayne's voice immediately and glanced across to where she was observing him over the fence.

"Hello, Miss Frayne. I see you haven't gone away this weekend."

"Oh, no, I very rarely do. As I explained, last weekend was quite an exception. Are you making good headway with the case?"

Chudd pulled a face. "Like most police work, it's a matter of slow, laborious, routine checking. There's nothing very dramatic or glamorous about it."

"No, I'm sure not. And such long hours, too, But it must have its rewards."

"Oh, it does, though they're not financial."

"I take it you're about to go into Mrs. Hibbert's house?" Miss Frayne's tone sounded full of hopeful interest.

"I just want to have another quick look around."

"In that case I wonder if I might ask you a favour? Could you bring out Nero's bowl? Unless anyone's touched it, it should be on the floor beneath the kitchen table. It has Nero painted on it. I think it would make him feel more at home if he could feed out of his own dish."

"How do you know about it?" Chudd asked suspiciously. "I understood you didn't have any truck with Mrs. Hibbert, yet you seem intimately acquainted with her cat's feeding habits."

Miss Frayne looked acutely embarrassed. "Now I know why you're a detective," she said, swallowing nervously. "I'm afraid I looked through the kitchen window the other evening and I saw the bowl with Nero's name then."

"So you've been prying, Miss Frayne," Chudd said severely.

"I wouldn't call it prying," she replied with a faint show of indignation. "I just thought I'd take a look round while I was there."

"And why were you there?"

"The fence has rotted a little at the far end and I could only get at it to put it right on Mrs. Hibbert's side."

"I see."

"I do assure you I was up to no harm," she went on hastily.

"I should hope not. But I suggest you don't do it again. The most innocent actions are liable to be misconstrued and, moreover, you were a trespasser."

"No, I'll be very careful in future," she said in a contrite voice.

"Well, if you wait here a moment, I'll fetch Nero's bowl now."

This would at least remove her excuse to hang over the fence all the while he was looking around inside. Not that he considered she would be in need of an excuse.

Using the front-door key of which the police had taken possession, he let himself into the house. Nero's bowl was, as Miss Frayne had seen it, beneath the kitchen table and he took it out immediately and handed it to her over the fence.

"Thank you so much, Inspector Chudd."

"Good-bye, Miss Frayne."

"Oh, I expect I'll see you when you leave. I shall still be in my garden."

Chudd refrained from reply, but went back inside the house. Closing the front door firmly behind him, he stood in the hall with eyes shut and tried to make his mind a blank. Then after standing in this fashion for a full minute, he opened his eyes and let his gaze flick about him. It was quite inconceivable that anyone could have been in the house and not have observed that there were clocks everywhere. You could see three from where he was standing in the hall and he knew there were at least two in every room. And yet Sherbrook had said he didn't notice the time because he didn't have a watch and hadn't seen a clock. Chudd tried to imagine whether even a youthful moron could have failed to notice such an abundance of horological reminders. The trouble was he did think it possible, given the right circumstances, namely if Sherbrook's mind – a not very high-powered instrument – had been concentrated solely on the achievement of his burglarious aims.

He climbed the stairs and entered Mrs. Hibbert's bedroom, which had a smell compounded of dust and stale eau de cologne. It always surprised him how rapidly a sealed and empty house took on the atmosphere of a provincial museum. Despite the grim association, he doubted whether Mrs. Mellor would have any difficulty in selling it, always assuming that this was her intention and that she wasn't proposing to live there herself.

Thinking of her reminded him that he was still waiting for information from Canada about the issue of her passport. She'd said that her previous one had expired some time earlier and that she'd been given an emergency one. But supposing it turned out that the previous one was still valid, her application for a fresh one could mean only one thing, namely that she had destroyed the other because it bore witness to a visit to England which she wished to conceal. A visit during which she had committed a murder and subsequently flown back across the Atlantic. It was an almost perfect alibi, but the case against her could be overwhelming if it were proved to be a false one. Her motive was the strongest of all. No one cares to be disinherited, and Jessie Mellor was, moreover, someone who might be ready to fight for her expected dues. At the moment, this was all supposition, but Chudd determined that given proof of one facet of the case against her, he would really burrow deep to establish evidence of the others.

On returning downstairs, he went into the living-room, and sat down at Mrs. Hibbert's writing desk. It was a small escritoire over in one corner, and though its contents had already been closely examined once, he decided to take a further look. But he found nothing to interest him. He knew from what he'd been told that she was a woman of strict habit and she'd obviously been a very orderly person into the bargain. This had resulted in her not keeping any letters, once presumably they'd been answered.

Chudd sighed. The hoarder who became the victim of crime, whether it was murder or fraud, was a much more fruitful source of clues than the obsessively tidy person who destroyed everything immediately it had served its purpose.

He did find an address book, but its data was entirely restricted to tradespeople in the Elwick Common district. Not even Mrs. Mellor's address was in it. Everything appeared to confirm that Mrs. Hibbert had lived a life of almost clinical detachment. But if that was a true picture of her, it seemed curious that she had accepted a lodger.

Chudd rose and walked slowly out into the hall. All he was achieving was to fill his mind with speculative thoughts, which were in danger of deflecting him from the path signposted by established facts. It was time he went.

As he closed the front-door behind him, Miss Frayne's head popped over the fence.

"Would you care to come in for a glass of sherry, Inspector? I usually have one myself on a Saturday evening and should be delighted if you would join me."

"That's very kind of you, Miss Frayne, but I mustn't stop. I promised my wife that I'd try and be home a little earlier this evening."

"What a pity! But of course I understand." She gave Mrs. Hibbert's house a meaning look. "Did you find out what you wanted or shouldn't I ask that question?"

"I was only poking around," he replied casually. Then before Miss Frayne could engage him in further conversation, he gave her a nonchalant wave and departed.

He called at the station to learn that there'd been no developments during his absence, and picking up his car drove home.

Kate was already in the kitchen surrounded by orderly chaos.

"We're having roast chicken," she said after he'd kissed her.

"With bread sauce, I hope."

"What with bread sauce for you, roast potatoes for David, stuffing for Andrew and crispy bacon for Timmy, the chicken hardly seems important."

"The trimmings are always the best part."

"And the most work for the cook."

"Can I give you a hand?" he enquired, glancing helplessly about him.

"No, you go and amuse the boys while I get on. It's ages since you played with them."

"Where are they?"

"Upstairs with the electric railway. At least David and Timmy are. I suspect Andrew has retired to his bedroom to read."

With his father's arrival, however, Andrew rejoined them, and during the next forty minutes their combined absorption was complete. Each of the boys was ready secretly to concede that the controlling presence of an adult was necessary if maximum enjoyment was to be obtained from operating their model train set. While, as for their father, he achieved blissful satisfaction from doing something with his sons.

The remainder of the evening was on a par and he went to bed feeling that his life had taken a turn for the better. When he mentioned this to Kate, she replied with light cynicism, "Don't imagine for one moment that it would be like that if you came home every evening at half past six."

"You mean you don't have bread sauce when I'm not here?"

She let out a giggle. "Sometimes we don't even have bread."

9

CHUDD woke up the next morning and decided that he was still in good spirits. After breakfast he bore his family off to church, and when the service finished left them to drop by the station.

A message had come through overnight from the Canadian

authorities saying that enquiries would be made into Jessie Mellor's passport situation, but that these might take a few days. Also forwarded were further particulars of her forgery conviction, and Chudd read this part of the cable with interest. It appeared that in 1952 when she had been working as housekeeper to a wealthy widower, she had made a practice of opening his mail and extracting any cheques. She had forged his name on these and cashed them, leaving his employ before the matter ever came to light. When it did, however, she was traced and arrested in a neighbouring province and brought to trial with the result already known. The message concluded by quoting a newspaper report which said that it had been a particularly mean and deliberate fraud on an old man who was physically infirm, as well as being partially blind.

Chudd read the cable through again. After all, it wasn't such a big step from forgery to murder where cupidity was the underlying motive in each instance. Nevertheless, the basic improbability in any case built up against Jessie Mellor was her knowledge that she was about to be cut out of her cousin's will – if indeed she was. She, of course, denied even knowing she was mentioned in it in the first place.

He was deep in thought when his telephone gave an unexpected ring. He glared at it resentfully and braced himself to lift the receiver. Supposing he was to become involved just when he was proposing to take the family out for the afternoon.

"Chudd here," he said in a cautious tone.

"Inspector Bracker wants to speak to you," said the officer on the switchboard.

"Put him through." What on earth could Bracker be phoning about on a Sunday morning? A second later, the inspector's rough-edged tones broke against his ear.

"They told me you were in so I supposed I'd better have a word with you. Thought you'd be taking Sunday off. I was only calling to find out if everything was all right. As well for someone to keep in touch over the weekend, but as you're there, I needn't have bothered."

Chudd decided to ignore the various innuendoes which were left trailing by Inspector Bracker's remarks. He declined to be drawn into a wrangle, but fancy being married to such a man! He had met Mrs. Bracker soon after his arrival at Elwick Common and had found her a colourless female with a muddy complexion. He understood there was a nineteen-year-old daughter who had left home after a row with her father and who had the reputation of being rather hot stuff.

By the time he reached home, Kate had packed a picnic and the boys were clamouring to be off. There followed the usual dispute as to whose turn it was to sit where in the car, but once this was settled they were away.

Looking back on it as they neared home some six hours later, Chudd reckoned it had been a successful outing. Everyone had found something to please him for part of the time, and that was the most which could be hoped for with three boys of mercurial changes of taste. David had the satisfaction of seeing Abbott, the captain of the school cricket side; Andrew had been content to read in the back of the car when he became bored with watching the polo and Timmy had been delighted by the presence of soldiers in uniform. As for him and Kate, it was sufficient to have spent an afternoon in the fresh air surrounded by nature's green.

As Chudd opened the front door, Timmy cried out, "There's a letter."

"Don't be daft, the postman doesn't deliver on Sundays," David said acidly.

"I never said it was a postman's letter."

"One of you pick it up and give it to me," Chudd broke in sharply, his hands being full of picnic equipment.

"It's for you, Dad and it's got urgent on it," David said, holding it out to his father.

Chudd put down his load and tore open the envelope. Inside on a sheet of office memo paper was written:

"Sir, Please ring when you get back. E. Dobson, P/Sgt. 3.50 p.m."

It was now nearly half past seven. He put through a call

immediately and was relieved when Sergeant Dobson himself answered the 'phone.

"It was the acting Governor of Bedford Prison, sir. He asked if you'd call him as soon as you came back."

"Did he say what about?"

"No, sir, except that it's to do with the murder. He said he wouldn't bother to explain it and that a few hours wait didn't matter. I have his number if you want to call him from home."

A few minutes later, Chudd was talking to Mr. Walls.

"Sorry to bother you on a Sunday, but I thought I'd better let you know that a Yale key has been found in Sherbrook's cell. I'm wondering whether it could be the one you're looking for?"

"Does it have a bit of red ribbon tied to the end?"

"No, nothing, but that could easily have come off. I imagine the only way you'll find out whether it's your key will be to try it in the lock. What would you like me to do about it?"

"I'll send somebody up for it immediately and if it does fit Mrs. Hibbert's door, I shall naturally want to see Sherbrook again."

"So I imagine."

"How was it found?"

"It's a somewhat involved story. We got wind through another prisoner that Billing and Sherbrook had some reefer cigarettes hidden in their cells so we decided to make a search. We didn't find any reefers but we did find the key."

"Where was it?"

"Beneath the mattress on his bed."

"Has he been questioned about it?"

"He doesn't even know we've got it. In case it turns out to be the key you're looking for, I thought you should have the pleasure of springing it on him. If it isn't, I'll have to hold a domestic enquiry as to its origin. Prisoners found in possession of keys make us a trifle nervous."

"How did this other prisoner come to know about the reefers – or to think he knew about them?"

"He's a notorious grass and Billing apparently said something to him on exercise which led him to believe they had some concealed in their cells."

"Do either Billing or Sherbrook know that their cells have been searched?"

"No."

"Was anything else found apart from the key?"

"Nothing illicit."

A minute later their conversation ended and Chudd immediately called the station to arrange for someone to drive up to the prison and collect the key. It was with considerable relief that he in fact discovered someone available to do so, as he'd faced the possibility of having to go himself. It would be three and a half to four hours before his emissary could be back and in the meantime nothing he could do, save wait patiently. It ran through his mind whether to warn Peggy Dunkley that she might be pulled out of bed to identify a key, but he decided against this. It was better that she should have no foreknowledge of what was happening.

About eleven o'clock, he left home and went to the station to await events.

The Detective Constable who had undertaken the mission arrived back at the station shortly before midnight. Waiting in his office, Chudd heard him coming up the stairs two at a time, and when he actually entered the room he might, from the sounds he was making, have run both ways. He handed Chudd a cheap manila envelope inside which a key could be plainly felt. Chudd tore off the end and shook the contents into the palm of his hand. Then picking up the one to Mrs. Hibbert's front door which he already possessed, he placed the one on top of the other.

"What's your verdict?" he asked the D.C. who had ceased to make noises like a beached whale.

"Looks identical to me, sir."

"To me, too. But there's only one way to be certain and that's try it in the door."

A near-by church clock was striking midnight as two shadowy figures walked up Mrs. Hibbert's front path. With the minimum of sound Chudd inserted the key and turned it. The door opened.

It was hard to realise in that moment that the case was at an end. There might still be loose ends to be tied, but doubt no longer remained about who had killed Mrs. Hibbert. And the solution was the one which he himself had been reluctant to accept. So Sherbrook's confession had been genuine after all.

"Come on, we must go and knock up Miss Dunkley," he said, closing the door behind him.

"She'll think you've come to arrest her, sir."

"Probably, but I can't help that."

But Peggy Dunkley was a sound sleeper and her new landlady deaf, so that it took several minutes to rouse anyone, by which time neighbours on either side had come to their windows and were peering out with uninhibited interest.

When Peggy Dunkley eventually appeared at the front door, her face was puffy with sleep and her hair gave her the appearance of a domestic slut.

"What on earth do you want?" she demanded angrily when she saw who the callers were.

"I'd like you to look at a key," Chudd said. "May we come in for a minute? It won't take longer, but we'll need some light."

Standing beneath the hall light, he held the key out for her to examine.

"Is it supposed to be my key to Mrs. Hibbert's front door?"

"I think it very well may be, even though the piece of red ribbon's been removed. Can you identify it any other way?"

She took it and turned it over with a doubtful expression.

"One Yale key's like another as far as I'm concerned."

"I hoped you might recognise it by some scratch or bit of tarnish, or something of that sort."

"Afraid I can't. I'm not saying it's not my key, but, equally, I certainly couldn't swear that it was. Where'd you find it?"

"I'm not a liberty to reveal that at the moment." He took the key from her and examined it carefully himself. "If you look very closely you'll see that the left prong of the Y in Yale is more worn than the other letters. Doesn't that help you? I'd ask you to think terribly carefully as this could turn out to be an absolutely vital point. Apart from the piece of red ribbon, wasn't there anything you ever noticed about your key?"

She frowned. "If I start thinking as hard as that, I'll only begin imagining things."

"I certainly don't want you to do that."

"But if you already have one key, this must be mine."

"How do you know for sure?"

"Because there were only two keys to the front door. She had one, I had the other."

"Can you be quite definite about that?" Chudd asked, his tone suddenly hopeful.

"Absolutely. I lost mine when I'd been there only a few months and she immediately had the lock changed and there were just the two keys. I have reason to remember it," she added with a sniff, "as Mrs. Hibbert made such a fuss about the whole affair and suggested that I should pay for having the new lock fitted."

"Do you happen to remember who supplied the new lock?"

"Poynter's in the High Street."

"Presumably they may still have a record or someone who'll recall the transaction," Chudd murmured.

"Possibly," Peggy Dunkley said in a frigid voice, "if you can't accept my word for it."

"It's not that. It's a question of evidence." He slipped the key into his pocket. "Thanks for your help, Miss Dunkley, and I apologise for having disturbed you at such an hour."

"I hadn't realised our police made nocturnal calls," she said with a tired smile. "I thought that sort of thing only happened in totalitarian countries."

"I've always understood that their visits are usually paid closer to dawn."

After leaving her, they drove back to the station where Chudd arranged for a car to pick him up at home at seven o'clock. He'd then be at the prison by half past eight or soon after, and from there he could 'phone the Deputy Commander and apprise him of the latest turn of events.

The charging of Sherbrook might be an end to the case in one sense, but it wouldn't in itself explain why Mrs. Hibbert had given Peggy Dunkley a false reason for her eviction or what changes in her will she had in mind. And Chudd still declined to believe that these were unrelated to her death. However, he'd have an opportunity to question Sherbrook further before he was actually charged.

It was twenty to two when he got into bed, and he set his alarm for six. Moreover, he knew from experience that the inside of his head was going to feel as if it'd been sand-papered when morning came. It always did when he went short of sleep. This was something to which his service had never accustomed him.

When at length he fell asleep it was to dream that Detective Inspector Bracker had been appointed head of the Soviet Secret Police and that Sherbrook, on being confronted with the key, snatched it out of his hand and swallowed it.

10

HE arrived at the prison the next morning feeling as gritty as he'd expected. His eyeballs had the sensation of having been rolled in sand and put back in again. The hour and a half drive had passed in a silence which had been punctuated only by the most laconic exchanges between himself and Detective Sergeant Roberts.

Sherbrook was plainly surprised to see them, and it was soon apparent that he'd had no inkling of their visit. When Chudd uttered the time-honoured words of the caution, an expression of cynical wariness came over his face.

"I want to ask you some questions about this key," Chudd said, producing it from his pocket and holding it up for Sherbrook to see.

"Well you won't get very far because I've never seen it before."

"You haven't looked at it properly yet." Sherbrook gave him a sharp glance and leaned forward to stare at it with a puzzled frown. "You know what this key is, don't you?"

"The one you asked me about the other night?"

"Exactly. And you know where it was found don't you?"

"Search me."

"Beneath the mattress in your cell."

Slowly Sherbrook raised his head until his eyes met Chudd's. His expression went suddenly blank and he said, "I'm saying nothing."

"It had a piece of red ribbon tied to the end when you took it, what happened to that?"

"I'm not saying any more."

"You're entitled not to, but since you've made a written confession of the murder I thought you might like to add a bit about the key."

"Well, I don't."

"You realise it clinches the case against you?"

"How do I know you're not trying to trick me?"

"There's nothing to trick you about. As I say, you've made a confession and now this has been found in your possession."

"Who searched my cell?"

"Prison officers, yesterday afternoon." There was a silence during which Sherbrook sat tight-lipped and frowning. "Well, is there nothing you wish to add?"

"I've already told you. I'm not saying anything."

"In that event, there's nothing more for me to say either, though I must warn you that you'll very likely be charged with the murder of Mrs. Hibbert within the next day or so."

After Sherbrook had been escorted from the room, the

acting Governor said, "I expected you to charge him now."

"I would have, but since there's to be a con with the D.P.P. later to-day, I thought it could await the outcome of that. It's not as though the bird can fly."

"What'll you do, charge him here and take him to court on a Home Office order?"

"Probably the other way about. Get him to court and charge him there."

"I have the impression that he may be about to retract his confession," the acting Governor remarked. "I can't think why he shouldn't otherwise have come clean about the key."

"He may try and retract it, I suppose, but he won't find it all that easy to do so, provided there's other evidence against him, such as the key."

"Nasty, vicious little brute. I'm still old-fashioned enough to think that his like who commit these senseless murders should finish up at the end of a rope."

Chudd glanced at his watch. "I wonder if I might use your 'phone and put through a call to the Yard?"

"Help yourself."

Deputy Commander Ellis sounded brisk and Monday-ish when Chudd came through to him. He listened without comment to what had happened and on conclusion said, "You'd better come straight here now and I'll try and fix a meeting at the Director's in a couple of hours' time or so."

"Does you boss approve of what you've done?" the acting Governor enquired amiably when Chudd replaced the receiver.

"I think one could say that judgment's reserved."

"I know, I know, it's results that count in your job."

"In most other people's, too," Chudd replied in a slightly nettled tone.

On the way back to London, he said to Sergeant Roberts, after a prodigious yawn, "What's the betting we don't see more of this road before the day is out?"

"Couldn't we get a helicopter?"

A few miles farther on, Chudd translated his thoughts into

words and asked abruptly, "Have you any further doubts about Sherbrook?"

"None, sir. I didn't have any before."

The remainder of their journey was accomplished in silence.

It was the first time since his transfer six weeks before that Chudd had set foot inside the Yard, and he found it rather like re-visiting a house in which one had once lived. Outwardly it was the same as it had always been, but the atmosphere now seemed different. He realised, of course, that the atmosphere was the same and that it was he who was different. He no longer belonged, he was a visitor. Nevertheless, it was pleasant to be greeted by several former colleagues as he and Detective Sergeant Roberts made their way along the corridors.

"Enjoying life out on Division, Peter?" one of them asked him heartily.

He could almost feel Sergeant Roberts waiting for his reply.

"Very much," he said stoutly. "Don't know how you people here manage to occupy your time."

"I'd tell you, except the building might catch light from spontaneous combustion."

Deputy Commander Ellis was waiting for them and jumped up as they entered his office.

"We have five minutes to get over to the D.P.P.'s place. I expected you sooner than this."

"We got caught up in traffic, sir."

"That's what my younger daughter always says when she arrives home at two in the morning."

Chudd smiled thinly. He remembered the girl in question as an extremely attractive twelve-year-old. She must now be around twenty. Police officers, it seemed, were prone to have daughters who turned out to be handfuls. Perhaps he was lucky to have only sons.

On the short drive to Buckingham Gate where the D.P.P. had his office, Chudd filled Mr. Ellis in with further details of Sherbrook's sudden eruption into the enquiry.

"Have you brought copies of his statement with you?"

"Yes, Sir."

The car drew up, and as he got out he said, "We'll now toss this little lot into the lawyers' laps and see what they say."

Chudd noticed that the conference room had been redecorated since he'd last been inside the building. A building which, despite its agreeable exterior and the plate by which it identified its august self, bore all the signs of being a government office once the threshold was crossed. The hideously mottled plastic floor tiles, the small clusters of moribund firebuckets, the black-streaked doors which had been opened by a thousand feet and the walls which were as smeared as an urchin's face, all proclaimed its functional purpose. The conference room on the first floor was, by contrast, gracious and inviting. It seemed a pity that visitors couldn't be taken to it blindfold so that they missed the utility horrors en route.

The Director took his seat at the head of the table with two of his staff on his right. The police officers sat on the opposite side. It was Detective Sergeant Roberts's first visit there and he sat uneasily on the edge of his chair. Chudd noticed this and was not displeased. Do him no harm to feel a bit of a country bumpkin. A second or two later, however, he was himself put out to find that a metal staple in his papers had caused a large scratch on the beautifully polished table and positively embarrassed when his efforts to remove this by a vigorous rub of his elbow attracted the Director's quizzical attention.

"I apologise for springing this on you without any warning," the Deputy Commander said, "but it's only blown up over the weekend and a decision is rather urgent."

"The decision being. . . . ? The Director asked mildly.

"Whether or not to charge this youth Sherbrook with the murder. I think the best thing would be for Chief Inspector Chudd to give you the brief background of the case and then show you the statement which Sherbrook has made."

All eyes turned for a moment on Chudd, who proceeded to outline the facts surrounding Mrs. Hibbert's death. He was listened to in silence as his audience relaxed into attitudes of attention. The Director's own watchful expression remained focused on him the whole time while one of his assistants doodled and the other bent paper-clips out of shape. The Deputy Commander sat back with arms folded across his chest and eyes fixed on the farthest skyline. Sergeant Roberts gave an impression of the concert pianist's assistant anxiously waiting to turn the music. As Chudd concluded his narrative, he handed round copies of the statement.

There followed a period of silence, then the Director said, "Well, I know what my own view is. This chap should be charged."

The Deputy Commander nodded. "I expected that to be your view," he remarked blandly.

"I don't see that you have any choice in the matter. It's neither your nor my responsibility to ignore a confession of this sort. We wouldn't have a leg to stand on in the face of any public criticism of a failure to charge Sherbrook on this evidence." He looked at the two senior members of his staff. "Don't you agree?"

"I do," said the paper-clip bender, firmly. "Even without the key, I'd say you'd have to charge him. It's not for us to weigh his statement. He may retract it, he could well be acquitted, anyway. But that's what courts are for. It'll be for a court to say whether the confession is to be believed or not, we can only take it at its face value." He fixed Chudd with an amiable smile. "It's not even as though you have evidence which contradicts the statement, in any material particular."

"That's largely because the statement is so vague and imprecise when it comes to detail," Chudd replied, marvelling at the manner in which his problem had been swiftly reduced to one simple issue.

"I don't know why you say that," the one who had been doodling now broke in. He proceeded to read out that portion of Sherbrook's statement in which he described how he had pulled the scarf tight round Mrs. Hibbert's neck until she went limp and how he'd then put the body beneath the bed. "Nothing very imprecise about that," he commented.

The point was unanswerable and Chudd made a small shrug

of acknowledgment. Why should he worry, anyway? He was content to have had the decision made for him and it wasn't one with which he had any wish to quarrel. It was one justified by the facts, and his own feelings of doubt about the case were irrelevant in the circumstances. Nevertheless, he felt stubbornly obliged to give the bone another gnaw.

"I still think it's curious that he refuses to say anything about the key."

"There could be several reasons for that," said the bender of paper clips, and then rather obviously set about trying to think of just one. "For example," he went on after a potent pause, "he may have had second thoughts and realised where this confession was likely to land him. In due course he'll try and retract it, but, for the time being, at least, he's not going to add to it. The aftermath of a confession is nothing like as stimulating as the actual moment of making it."

"You seem to speak with great authority," his colleague observed drily.

"I do. I remember owning up at school, to being the boy who'd put a toad in the matron's bed. It was an exploit which had received the accolade of everyone's approval, except the matron's, and I had the additional satisfaction of confessing in front of the whole school. It was a wonderful moment, though between then and bedtime, which was the hour set for my punishment, I would have given anything to have been able to retract. In the interval it became clear that the headmaster viewed the incident far more grimly than I'd expected when I'd stood up and hogged the limelight. Mind you, I didn't think he'd publicly join in the laughter, but I can tell you I was terrified out of my wits when he made the sombre announcement that he proposed to beat me in front of the whole school. Such a thing had never happened before and probably never has again." He chuckled at the recollection. "Your Master Sherbrook could be going through something of the same sort, the initial excitement of his confession having worn off."

A ruminative silence followed, then the Deputy Commander said, "What does anyone make of the false reason which Mrs.

Hibbert gave to get rid of her lodger? I know Chief Inspector Chudd would appreciate your views on that, too."

"Coincidence," said the paper-clip bender. "It has to be coincidence. And after all, why not, life's full of them."

"It certainly seems unrelated to her death," the Director said judicially. "It wouldn't be the first time that a large red herring was trailed across the path of a murder enquiry."

"I think Inspector Chudd's point is that there are too many apparent red herrings for them all to be dismissed as coincidences," the Deputy Commander remarked. "Though my own view is the same as yours" – he nodded in the direction of the paper-clip man – "When you put life under the microscope, as happens in the course of criminal investigation, you find it seething with coincidences, red herrings, crossed paths and all the rest."

Chudd gave a resigned nod. "Perhaps I am in danger of not seeing the wood for the trees."

"You have an admirably charted wood in the shape of Sherbrook's statement coupled with the finding of the key," said the doodler, looking up with a small smile.

Shortly after this the meeting broke up and the three officers returned to the Yard. From there Chudd made a number of telephone calls, the effect of which was to arrange for Sherbrook to be brought to Elwick Common Magistrates' Court the next morning where he was to be charged with the murder. His final call was to the station to inform Inspector Bracker of the decision which had been taken.

"I should think so, too," he had said in a tone to indicate his view that too many people had been wasting their time on a perfectly clear issue.

Chudd didn't telephone the court, deciding that it would be better to call in there on his way back and see Mr. Rome, the clerk, personally. Elwick Common Magistrates' Court was not one of the easiest with which to have dealings from anyone's point of view. Defendants, witnesses, lawyers and police were each in their turn subjected to the scourging irritability and impatience of Mr. Bristow, the presiding stipendiary, and to the pernicketiness of Mr. Rome, which could be almost as frustrating. The only difference between them was that whereas Mr. Rome was basically a kindly man, Mr. Bristow had no such pretensions. He was pompous, rude and unable to accept that anyone in his court was able to do their job as well as he could do it for them. He applied this maxim as much to his clerk as to all the rest who had the misfortune to appear before him.

Those who were able to take a more detached view opined that he was a sick man. Chudd couldn't help feeling, however, that sick men shouldn't hold jobs where the freedom of others depended on the hour to hour state of someone else's internal organs. Even though justice might reasonably often be achieved in Mr. Bristow's court, it very seldom gave the appearance of so being done.

Mr. Rome listened to Chudd with a prim expression and his fingertips pressed together.

"So you will be asking for a formal seven-day remand tomorrow?"

"Yes."

"And when will the prosecution be ready to open?"

"The police have almost completed their enquiries, but of course we have to get a file to the Director."

"In about two weeks, say?"

"Perhaps three."

Mr. Rome studied a list beneath the slab of glass which covered the top of his desk. "Mr. Bristow will be away three weeks from now so we can't fix a date then."

Chudd wanted to ask why his replacement shouldn't deal with the case, but the clerk answered this as though he could read his thoughts.

"He won't be willing to relinquish this case to the relief magistrate." He picked up a highly sharpened pencil and made a note in a large diary.

"There'll be no question of your asking this court to hear the other charge as well?"

"No. It's not connected in any way with the murder. I

imagine the Bedford police will ask for it to be adjourned sine die in the circumstances."

"How it's disposed of is not my concern, as long as you assure me that no one will try and suggest we should deal with it. And how long will the case last when it begins? I must have some idea of the length if I'm to make suitable arrangements."

"I would say that it can be completed comfortably in a day."

"You're sure of that? Some people's estimates of the time which cases will take are extraordinarily unrealistic."

"I can't see it lasting longer than a day," Chudd replied evenly.

"You don't sound too certain. How many witnesses will you be calling?"

"I can't tell you at this stage. That'll be the Director's decision, and as I mentioned he hasn't yet received our file."

"But surely you can give me some idea?"

"A dozen perhaps, but that's no better than a guess."

Mr. Rome let out a small exasperated sigh and wrote something further in the diary. "Anything else of help you can tell me about the case?" Chudd shook his head, but Mr. Rome went on, "Interpreter required?"

"No."

"Many documentary exhibits?"

"Photos, plan and accused's statement. I can't think of any others."

"No witnesses who may wish to swear obscure oaths?"

"None that I know of."

"Well, that seems to be all then," he said, closing the diary with a flourish as if it were a well-filled order book. He gave Chudd a quizzical smile. "How are you enjoying Elwick Common after the Yard?"

"It's a stimulating change."

"I suppose that could be so," Mr. Rome said in a doubtful voice. "This'll be your first major case with us since you came, won't it?"

"Yes, it will."

"I trust it'll be a pleasurable experience."

Chudd smiled mechanically. He hoped so, too, but felt it was unlikely.

II

CHUDD was waiting at court the next morning when the car which had been sent to fetch Sherbrook arrived. He was present when the uniformed court inspector formally charged him with murder, as they stood in a small huddle in the passage which led from the jailer's office to the half dozen cells. Sherbrook shook his head when asked if he wished to say anything in answer to the charge. The court inspector turned on his heel and the jailer escorted Sherbrook to a cell to await his appearance in court. Chudd stood uncertainly for a second, then went back into the office.

Detective Sergeant Roberts, who had made the journey with Sherbrook, came in from the yard.

"Did he say anything on the way down?" Chudd enquired.

"Nothing of any consequence, sir. He was in what you might call a silent mood. He didn't even register much when I told him he was going to be brought here and charged. Though I suppose it can't have come as any surprise to him after our visit yesterday." Sergeant Roberts scratched at an ear. "I had thought he might show a bit of interest when we were driving through Elwick Common but he didn't give off so much as a flicker." He studied the finger with which he had been scratching the ear. "All he wanted to know was whether he'd be returning to Bedford Prison and I told him he'd probably go to Brixton."

"I had a further talk with Superintendent Smith about that this morning," Chudd said. "He intends to ask the court to dispose of the charge against Billing tomorrow, and he thinks they'll probably commit for sentence. Moreover there's the question of his Borstal licence to be considered. Anyway I agreed that they couldn't hold up Billing's case indefinitely and that there was no reason why it shouldn't be dealt with separately as far as we were concerned."

The jailer's office was filling up and assuming an air of feverish activity. The prison van from Brixton had just arrived and decanted three prisoners. Others who'd been on bail were being claimed with obvious relief by police officers. The telephone was in constant use, being frequently handed over the tops of heads and thrust between conversing couples. The whole atmosphere was that of a corner of the Stock Exchange as the market crashed. Suddenly over the top of the rising hubbub a voice called out, "Quiet in there, he's on the bench." And quiet surprisingly fell, those who still had problems to resolve taking themselves off to the remoter purlieus.

Chudd slipped through the door which led into the court-room and went and squeezed himself into the small pen occupied by the court inspector. He was aware of Mr. Bristow giving him an unfriendly glance as he sat down.

Mr. Bristow was a short, wiry man with a head of beautifully tended silvery hair, and on his nose a pair of half-glasses which served to emphasize his expression of disdain for the world around him.

The usual round of applications was coming to an end and the magistrate was looking about him as though daring anyone else to step forward and demand his attention.

"Do you have an application, Inspector?" Mr. Rome said in the direction of the court inspector who that moment had turned to whisper something into Chudd's ear.

Mr. Bristow tapped his pencil petulantly. "Kindly do me the courtesy of not conducting your conversations in my court."

The court inspector rose as though he'd sat on a hornet.

"I apologise, your worship," he stammered unhappily. "I

apply for fifty police summonses in respect of speeding and parking offences."

"Very well, your application is granted, "Mr. Bristow said in a tone of distaste.

"I'm much obliged, your worship."

"I'm sure you realise that this court is already vastly over-worked and that there's a limit to the number of these motoring cases I can deal with. It's high time other arrangements were made." He cast a poisonous glance at Mr. Rome. "Yes, well let's get on, what are we waiting for! I have a very heavy list this morning."

The jailer scurried out to bring in the first charge.

"Charge number one, Sir, Horace Jones," he announced breathlessly a few seconds later.

Mr. Rome had just begun to read out the charge when Mr. Bristow stopped him.

"There's someone chewing in the public gallery. You," he called out to a pimply youth whose jaws had ground to an abrupt halt, "this is a court, not a cafe. If you wish to eat, kindly go outside."

The youth stared stolidly back at him but made no effort to move, and Mr. Bristow turned back to his register with an officious frown.

Mr. Rome had just begun to re-read the charge when Mr. Bristow's head went up like an angry rhino's disturbed at feeding-time. "There's far too much noise outside. If I can't have absolute quiet, I'll clear the whole building. It's quite intolerable being expected to concentrate hour after hour in conditions resembling an oriental market." He glared at the court inspector. "Kindly do something about it, Inspector."

Eventually, after Mr. Bristow had made several further interventions and complained once more about the length of his list, Horace Jones was able to plead guilty to having been drunk the night before and to be guided out to pay his fine.

"There don't appear to be any windows open at all," Mr. Bristow said crossly. "I don't know how one's supposed to work in such an atmosphere."

"We shut the windows, sir, because of the noise," the court inspector explained.

"So I either have to suffocate or be deafened," the magistrate remarked. This time, no one attempted to make any reply.

"Charge number four, sir, Ronald Sherbrook," announced the jailer, giving Chudd a surreptitious wink.

Chudd slipped from his seat and stepped into the witness-box.

"In this case, your worship . . . . ." he began, when Mr. Bristow, who had been poring over his register, looked up sharply.

"One moment, officer. Can't you see I'm not ready." He transferred his look to the jailer. "What has happened to charges two and three?"

"I thought we'd get Mr. Chudd's case out of the way, sir. Two and three are for hearing and his is going over." The jailer, who was shortly due to retire, had never yet been rattled by Mr. Bristow and was wont to say with a laugh, "Just treat him like you would your mother-in-law."

"It'll be for me to say whether his case goes over or not," Mr. Bristow said icily, at which the jailer gave Chudd another wink. The magistrate turned toward the witness-box. "Well, what is your application in this matter?"

"For a remand, sir. This man was only charged at the rear of this court this morning."

"I didn't ask for a case history. What length of remand are you asking for?"

"Seven days, though a further one will be necessary."

"I'd be obliged, Chief Inspector, if you'd confine yourself to the questions I put to you. It is not your role to tell me whether further remands will be necessary. You may apply for such, but their necessity will be for me to assess."

Chudd assumed a blank expression and remained silent, and Mr. Bristow, glaring at Sherbrook over the top of his half-lenses, said, "You have heard the police application, have you anything to say why you should not be remanded in custody for seven days?"

"I'd like legal aid."

"Nobody's mentioned legal aid to this moment. Kindly answer my question."

"What question?"

"Is there any reason why I shouldn't remand you in custody for seven days?"

"Don't suppose so."

"Then that is what I propose to do."

"Now, do I understand that you're applying for legal aid?"

"That's right."

The magistrate turned to Chudd. "Does he have any money?"

"None to speak of, sir."

Mr. Bristow threw down his pencil. "How much more expeditiously the work of this court could be conducted if people would only answer the questions which are put to them." Snapping the words as though they were matchsticks, he repeated. "Does the accused have any money?"

"Four pounds sixteen shillings and twopence."

Someone at the back of the Court tittered and Mr. Bristow raked the area with a ferocious glare.

"Then I shall grant you legal aid and remand you in custody for seven days."

Outside the courtroom, the jailer grinned at Chudd. "Twenty minutes to deal with two charges that should have lasted thirty seconds each."

"No wonder he feels overworked," Chudd observed grimly.

"Oh, there's another reason for that. He never comes on the bench before twenty to eleven and he's off home by five past four come hell or high water. He works fewer hours in a week than you do in a day. Ah well, time to return to the battle front. Here you, James Maitland Crossthwaite – cor what a name – it's your turn for the chopping block. Look lively."

The jailer and his next charge passed through the swing door into court. Chudd was just about to light his pipe when the assistant jailer had who been locking Sherbrook in his cell returned to the office and said, "He wants to have a word with you."

154

Chudd put the pipe back into his pocket and followed the assistant jailer back to the cells. Sherbrook was sitting on the edge of the wooden shelf which passed for a bed and made no attempt to get up when Chudd was ushered in.

"What's wrong with that old bugger?" he asked belligerently.

"If you're referring to the magistrate, he's always like that."

"A real old sod, isn't he!"

"I understand you wanted to speak to me," Chudd said, ignoring not without difficulty the invitation to vilify Mr. Bristow.

"Got a cigarette?"

"No, I smoke a pipe, but I'll see you get some before you leave."

Sherbrook bit his lower lip and glanced furtively around the cell.

"Yeh, I did want to speak to you." His tone was abstracted and distant.

"Well?"

He suddenly swung round and fixed Chudd with a hard stare. "It wasn't me what killed the old girl," he said fiercely. "And that's the truth."

12

FOR a full minute Chudd stood looking down at Sherbrook in silent appraisal, trying to decide how he should react to the volte-face. He found that he wasn't particularly surprised by it, nor even perturbed at the prospect of re-opening certain aspects of the enquiry. This would be inevitable whatever the disclosures Sherbrook would now be obliged to make, whether they appeared to be without substance or otherwise.

"So you didn't kill her, eh?" he said quietly.

"No."

"Even though you've made a signed written confession."

"It wasn't true."

"A jury may decide that it is."

"But they can't . . ."

"Especially when it's coupled with the finding of the key in your cell."

"I didn't know nothing about the key. I'd never seen it before."

"That again will be something for the jury to decide."

"The bloody key was planted on me. It must have been."

"Who by?"

"By Billing, of course. It was him who murdered the old girl."

"I suppose he told you all this?" Chudd enquired in a faintly sarcastic tone.

"Yes, he did. He told me he'd gone to the house and killed her."

"Why had he killed her?"

"She found him taking something."

"Let's get this straight, Sherbrook. What you're saying is that you've adopted Billing's account of what took place."

"Yes."

"You're going to have an uphill task persuading anyone of that. However, what made you confess to someone else's murder?"

A sulky look came over Sherbrook's face. "They was getting at me, making out I couldn't even steal an ice-cream from a sleeping kid without making a mess of it. I just blurted it out to make them take notice. It was that young screw who kept picking on me."

"And what's suddenly decided you to change your mind?"

"The key. Billing's try to frame me. He must have slipped it into my cell some time. I'm not taking the rap for him."

Chudd sighed. The logic of Sherbrook's mind eluded him. "But that's just what you were prepared to do when you made that written confession."

"Yea, but I could always deny that. The key was a deliberate plant on his part. He was trying to stitch me up proper."

"Even if it's true, he was only helping with a job you'd started yourself."

"He was trying to frame me with that key," Sherbrook repeated stubbornly.

"Supposing the key had not been found in your cell, how long were you proposing to wait before going back on your statement."

"I don't follow you."

"I presume you've had it in mind to retract your statement at some stage, when were you proposing to do so?"

"During my trial."

"Leaving it a bit late, weren't you?"

Sherbrook looked puzzled. "What d'you mean?"

"The jury might have accepted the statement as true."

"They couldn't have. They can't nail you just on your own word if you later say it isn't true."

"Who says they can't?"

"Everyone knows that."

"Is that something you've picked up?"

"Well, it's true, isn't it?"

"It may often work out that way in practice, but there's no rule of law about it."

"But finding the key definitely made things worse for me?"

"It certainly *has*."

The tense was not lost on Sherbrook. "But surely you believe me? You've got to believe me. It's the truth."

Chudd looked at him pityingly. "I wouldn't believe you if you told me December the twenty-fifth was Christmas Day, unless I could check it on a calendar."

"What are you going to do then? I want to make a fresh statement, I . . ."

"Just listen a moment," Chudd broke in. "When your

solicitor comes to see you, you'd better tell him everything you've told me and he'll advise you what to do."

"But aren't you going to charge Billing?"

"What I'm going to do is none of your business. As far as I'm concerned you're charged with the murder and you're in the custody of the court, and you're going to spend the next seven days stewing in Brixton Prison. I'm not responsible for your welfare any longer."

He turned and left the cell with Sherbrook picking nervously at a spot on the side of his chin. Before driving back to the station, he ascertained the name of the solicitor who would be assigned to the defence. It was Mr. Winters, of whom Chudd knew little save that he had a reputation for amiability and for managing to remain genial even when kicking someone in the teeth.

On reaching the station his first telephone call was to the solicitor, who received news of his assignment with equanimity.

"And why are you the bearer of these tidings, Chief Inspector?" he enquired.

"I was coming to that," Chudd replied, and then related to him what had happened after Sherbrook's appearance in court.

"So what are you suggesting I do?" the solicitor asked through what sounded like a smothered yawn when Chudd had finished.

"I'm not making any suggestions, I'm just putting you in the picture."

"And a pretty horrible one, too, if I may say so. Ah, well, thanks for letting me know. I'd better see my client as soon as possible, I suppose. Meanwhile what will you be doing about all this?"

"Enquiring into it," Chudd said non-committally.

"And if you find evidence to justify my client's immediate release, I imagine you will let me know?"

"That'll be a matter for the Director. It'll be for him to decide whether the proceedings against Sherbrook go ahead or whether no evidence is offered. It'll hardly be the latter unless it becomes incontestably clear that Billing really is the murderer."

"What's your view on that?"

"As far as I'm concerned, your chap has been charged on perfectly good evidence and there'll have to be something strong to displace it."

"That seems to be that then," Mr. Winters remarked affably. "We shall doubtless be in touch with each other quite soon,"

As soon as Mr. Winters was off the line, Chudd was told that Mr. Dann was waiting to speak to him. Mrs. Hibbert's solicitor's pedantic tones quickly dissipated the easy-going air engendered by Mr. Winters.

"Mrs. Mellor wishes to visit the house. I take it you have no objection?"

"Do you mean Mrs. Hibbert's house?"

"Naturally! What other could I possibly mean?"

"Will you be accompanying her?"

"One of my clerks will."

"I think a police officer ought to be present."

"Are you frightened Mrs. Mellor will destroy evidence or misconduct herself in some way?" Mr. Dann asked sarcastically.

"Not at all, but as the house has been sealed since her death and our enquiries are not yet complete, I think it would be in everyone's interest for one of my men to be present at Mrs. Mellor's visit. One doesn't want it to become the subject of adverse comment later. The defendant's legal advisers might be able to make a false point out of it, so it would be as well to avoid such a possibility."

"Very well," Mr. Dann said coldly. "I have no wish to make an issue of the matter, so I'll agree to your terms. I'll explain to Mrs. Mellor that it is customary practice over here and we will hope that she understands."

Chudd wanted to reply that he didn't mind whether Mrs. Mellor understood or not. He saw her only as a predatory female who'd come winging post haste across the Atlantic to lay claim to her inheritance. An inheritance which a week later *might* not have been hers. If only Mrs. Hibbert had somewhere left a clue as to how she'd been proposing to change her will. He liked to believe that the case would have been solved by now if she had done so. Really solved, that is, not merely with a solution imposed on a tangle of loose ends, rather like a lid on an over-crammed box of used string.

After finishing with Mr. Dann, he put through a call to the Deputy Commander who listened in silence and then said bleakly, "You'll have to see Billing straightaway, and after that we'll probably need a further conference along the road. That is, unless you've heard by then from his solicitor that Sherbrook has retracted his retraction."

It was half past two when Chudd arrived outside the now familiar main gate of Bedford Prison. He had Detective Inspector Bracker with him on this occasion and, in the absence of their usual C.I.D. driver, they had shared the driving to enable each to swallow some food on the way. Chudd found himself quite unreasonably irritated by the noisy manner in which Bracker masticated his cold roast beef sandwich and saw this as confirmation that the gulf between them was unbridgeable. Bracker spent the greater part of the journey denouncing an all-embracing, if ill-defined, "they".

Terry Billing gave the same impression of wary detachment as he had done the last time Chudd had interviewed him. He sat down on the chair which was offered him as though he'd been called in for consultation and was granting a favour.

"I'll come to the point at once," Chudd said. "Your mate, Sherbrook, has gone back on his confession of the murder of Mrs. Hibbert."

Billing smiled faintly. "That doesn't surprise me! Incidentally, the fact that we were arrested together, doesn't make him my mate."

"Why doesn't it surprise you?" Chudd asked, suspiciously.

"Because he's all imagination. I was only with him a couple of days but I discovered that pretty soon."

"He says you murdered her," Chudd went on, watching him intently.

Billing gave him a tolerant smile. "So I'd guessed."

"You'd guessed?"

"Why else should you come and see me? It's none of my

business that Sherbrook's gone back on his statement, unless he's also tried to bring me into it. Obvious, isn't it?"

"And what's your answer?"

"To deny it. Completely."

"Why should he have made the accusation?" Bracker broke in aggressively.

Billing looked at him in surprise. "Fairly obvious, isn't it? When you're in as deep as he is, you clutch at any straw, and I just happen to be a handy straw."

"He says," Chudd went on, before Bracker could interrupt again, "that his confession was based entirely on what you'd told him and that it was your confession to him which, in effect, he adopted as his own."

"Absolute cock! Do you believe that if I'd murdered the old woman, I'd have told that little runt what I'd done?"

"You might have."

"Well, I didn't. Didn't murder her. It was he who told me that he'd killed her."

"That isn't exactly what you said last time."

"Not all at once it wasn't, because I didn't want to grass; but once I realised he'd spilt the beans himself, I confirmed what he'd told you."

Chudd recognised that this was true as he recalled how he had extracted from Billing bit by bit what amounted to corroboration of Sherbrook's own confession.

"One of you's obviously lying," Inspector Bracker said. "He says you did it and you say he did."

"I've never said anything of the sort," Billing replied indignantly. "I've only repeated what he told me. I don't know whether he murdered her or not. I wasn't present at her death."

"You think you're pretty clever, don't you? You're obviously one of those barrack-room lawyer types, who believes he knows all the answers. Well, I advise you not to try and act Mr. Clever Boy with us. I repeat that either you or Sherbrook is lying and we shall find out soon enough which it is."

Chudd who had listened to Bracker's diatribe with concealed irritation now said, "Supposing you were called to give evidence, would you repeat in court what Sherbrook said to you?"

"You can leave me out of it."

"It may become necessary to call you as a witness, however, so what then?"

Chudd knew that the lawyers would very likely be asking him this question and realised that much might hang on his answer. It was therefore important that he should reach a firm assessment of Billing's reliability as a potential witness. After all, if Billing was to be believed, his evidence afforded vital corroboration of what Sherbrook subsequently told the police. In an era when juries were inclined to look askance at confessions made to the police, albeit in writing and signed, the fact that they'd been repeated to someone else as well could be very important. The trouble here was that the someone else was himself of dubious reputation, and the D.P.P. would have to be one hundred per cent satisfied not only that he was telling the truth, but that he would come up to proof at the required time.

"You can't force me to give evidence," Billing said warily. "But if I were to help you, what would you do for me in return?"

"I can't strike any bargains with you," Chudd replied, though the suggestion came as no surprise to him. He realised, however, that any discussion of terms on which Billing might be ready to testify would be adding a stick of dynamite to the case.

Billing shrugged. "You can't expect me to grass on him, and that's what I'd be doing if I gave evidence."

"But you'd be ready enough to grass if the price were sufficient," Bracker observed in a hectoring tone.

Billing gave a further shrug, and, with it, provided Chudd with his answer.

As the two officers left the prison, Bracker, who had shown signs of restiveness toward the end of the interview, turned to Chudd and said bleakly, "I don't know why you didn't put it to him that they were both in on the old woman's death."

"In the first place there's not a shred of evidence to suggest that and in the second, even if I had thought of it, it would clearly have drawn a blank denial."

"Nevertheless, it's obvious to me that's the way it was. I'm not saying that the actual murder was a joint affair. It probably wasn't, but it's my guess that the other one was present in the house and probably helped afterwards with the body."

"And which of them did do the murder?" Chudd asked, as a matter of formality.

"Sherbrook, I'd say. He's the more vicious, unstable type. And having done something which he felt earned him a medal, he had to boast about it. At the outset he plainly didn't want to share the limelight with anyone, but now he's begun to have cold feet and so he's split on Billing, who's a much shrewder youth and who was quite content for his mate to carry the whole can. Billing must have quietly laughed himself sick when he found out that Sherbrook had confessed to the whole thing single-handed. It was better than a plateful of his favourite nosh."

"One thing is certain," Chudd remarked, "we can never call Billing as a prosecution witness."

"That's why I'd put him in the dock as well and let them cut each other's throats."

"But we would have to have evidence before we could charge Billing," Chudd said impatiently, "and there isn't any."

"Yet. It's our job to unearth some." Though he said *our*, his tone clearly implied *your*. "For instance, what about finger-prints?"

"What about them? The only distinguishable prints found at the house were the dead woman's, Peggy Dunkley's and Stack's."

"Were there no others at all?"

"None that could be used for identification purposes," Chudd replied gratingly.

"Have Billing's prints been referred to our fingerprint people?"

"Yes, and Sherbrook's."

"I only asked. It isn't my fault that I'm not fully in the

picture. I've had other work to attend to as well, and you made it fairly clear at the beginning that you didn't welcome anyone's advice."

Chudd chose to ignore this remark. It would have been easy to have joined issue with him and to have embarked on a first-class row, but he had little doubt that, if he did so, he would be the one to suffer the worst effects. Not because he would feel he'd been in the wrong, but because he was aware of the subsequent turmoil rowing always left in him. Whereas, Bracker, he felt sure, could engage in a quarrel and emerge mentally unscathed. He was wrapped in a thick skin of leathery arrogance which shielded him against the opinions of others.

As soon as they reached the station, Chudd telephoned the Deputy Commander and gave him his conclusions.

"Well, it'll be for the Director to decide what to do about Billing," Mr. Ellis said, when he had finished. "I don't see how we can put him forward as a witness of truth. On the other hand, I can see the defence using his absence as an excuse to throw dust in the jury's eyes."

"The defence'll have it both ways. Criticise us if we do call him and throw out all manner of dark hints if we don't."

"You're probably right. Of course, there's nothing to prevent their calling him if they wish."

"They certainly won't do that unless he'll stand up and say "I did it'."

"Not much hope of that, I gather." The Deputy Commander let out an exasperated snort. "I always hate these cases which are overhung with unresolved question marks. Even when one's satisfied that they're not relevant to the main issue, putting this across to a jury is quite a different matter. I can just see the defence in this case dangling Billing's name in front of them at every opportunity, and we shall be powerless to do anything about it."

"Our rules of evidence are not designed to extract the whole truth of any matter," Chudd said, seizing the opportunity to air one of his professional grievances. "Their aim is only to ensure so-called fair play in proving someone's guilt."

The Deputy Commander let out a further snort. "You've been reading books." After a pause he added, "However, whatever the outcome about Billing, you'll have to be ready to give an assessment of the part he played. Not in evidence, of course, but for the information of counsel and, possibly also, of the judge in due course. Whether Sherbrook is ever convicted or not, someone is going to ask an awful lot of questions once he points his nasty finger at Billing. It could be Evans and Christie all over again, except that our two will still both be alive. Anyway, I'll let the Director's people know the latest position. If they want any further information, they'd better 'phone you direct."

A few minutes later Chudd was informed that Mr. Winters was below and would like to have a word with him. When the solicitor came into the room, he walked straight over to Chudd's desk and with an air of faint amusement deposited a foolscap envelope.

"You will find inside that, Chief Inspector, a copy of my client's further statement."

"Already?" Chudd asked.

"In the light of what you said to me, I thought I'd better go and see him at the court, before he was taken off to Brixton. This is the result." Observing Chudd's somewhat wary expression, he went on. "It doesn't contain any new shocks. Reading it won't send your blood pressure up. It consists of a retraction of his first statement and of a denunciation of Billing as the murderer – or rather as the person who told my client that he was the murderer, which is perhaps slightly different."

The qualification had a familar ring. It was only two hours before that Billing had made the same point when Sherbrook's confession was under discussion.

Leaving the envelope unopened before him, Chudd asked "Does he give any further reason for having made a false confession in the first place?"

Mr. Winters shook his head. "No, but a psychiatrist may be able to explain that, if it becomes necessary. By which I mean, if we have to stand trial." There was a pause and then Winters said smoothly, "Personally, I'm inclined to believe my client's story. His conduct fits into a well-recognised pattern." He ran a finger around his chin. "Do we yet know Billing's response?"

"Yes. A flat denial."

"I suppose that was to be expected. So what has been decided?"

"Nothing. It's too soon for a decision to have been made."

"So you can't say what Billing's position in all this is going to be."

"No."

"I'd like to know as soon as a decision is reached. As you can realise, the defence will be vitally interested."

"I'll let you know something as soon as I can."

"Mmm. I'll probably 'phone the D.P.P.'s office myself, too."

"A good idea."

Winters appeared to be lost in thought, but looking up suddenly he said with an amused smile, "Messy case, isn't it?"

"Very."

"But at least not a dead one from the defence point of view as so many are. Counsel could have some fun with this one."

"At whose expense?"

Mr. Winters laughed. "That remains to be seen. But the police are not the only people to have brickbats thrown at them. It happens to solicitors as well. A young man, whom I defended and got off a few weeks ago, is complaining because I referred to him in court as being under the evil influence of the girl he was going around with at the time. As a result of this, he says his manhood has been impugned and he's having difficulty in dating girls which he never experienced before."

After Winters had departed, Chudd pulled out Sherbrook's statement and read it. There were, indeed, no surprises in it. It merely confirmed the impasse which had developed as a result of his being charged.

Sherbrook, Billing. Billing, Sherbrook. As far as Chudd was concerned, the presence of neither helped to explain the matters which continued to puzzle him. It was as though he was trying to join together the halves of two different cases: to impose a solution which just didn't fit the facts. Except that it was a solution which had imposed itself with Sherbrook's confession – a solution which Chudd's mind had been rejecting ever since rather as the body's mechanism rejects what it can't absorb.

It was while he was contemplating the now well-worn paths of the enquiry that the telephone rang.

"D.C. Embler here, sir," a rather distant voice announced.

"Where the hell are you speaking from?"

"A public call box in the Strand, sir. I'm afraid it's not a very good connection."

"You'd better get on and say your piece before someone saws right through the line."

"I've found out the name of Mrs. Hibbert's sister who was killed in a car crash with her husband. It was Billing."

13

IF D.C. Embler had been standing in front of him, Chudd thought he might well have hugged him, such was the suffusion of well-being which reached suddenly to every nerve end in his body. He was almost numb with satisfaction, as happens with the receipt of tidings as unexpected as they are welcome. It required a conscious effort to re-focus his mind on what Embler was saying.

"I've just come from Somerset House, sir, where I was finally able to confirm what I'd discovered elsewhere. I've been on a real old treasure hunt, sir, but official records were the end of the quest."

Chudd could tell that Embler was himself bursting with pleasure at his achievement.

"You've done a splendid job unearthing this," he said. "Give me a few more details before you come back."

"The important detail, as you'll have guessed, is that the Billings had a son who was christened Terence. He was born on the fourth of November nineteen forty-four at Gainsborough in Lincolnshire."

"How did you manage to get on to the name?"

"That's quite a story, sir. I found out that Mr. Hibbert, when he was alive, was a staunch rotarian and that he had a particular friend there called Mr. Penrich, who is still alive. So I went to see Mr. Penrich and I asked him if he'd ever heard Mr. Hibbert mention a motor accident in which his sister-in-law and her husband had been killed. I said it would have been around nineteen fifty. Mr. Penrich said he couldn't remember any dates but he did recall Mr. Hibbert telling him of such an event. The two things which stuck in his mind were that Mr. Hibbert said his wife had never got on with her sister and hadn't seen her for years and therefore it hadn't been the terrible shock it otherwise would have been. But more particularly he remembered the place where the accident had happened because it had been a few miles from where he was born, which was Banbury.

"Armed with that information, I spent most of yesterday in the British Museum newspaper room looking through back files of the local paper. There were a good many fewer cars on the road in nineteen fifty and correspondingly fewer accidents, and, anyway, there aren't all that number involving the simultaneous deaths of a husband and wife. There were only three reported for the whole of that year, the third being of Albert and Catherine Billing, and in the report about them was mentioned the fact that they were survived by a five-year-old son. All that was left then was to check the name of the son in the records at Somerset House."

"That's a really great job," Chudd said admiringly. "It's thanks to you that some light's been finally shed on this case." He smiled wryly to himself as he recalled the circumstances in which he had sent D.C. Embler off on that particular expedition. It had been something in the nature of a punitive assignment, following their visit to Mrs. Mellor at her Kensington Hotel.

So Terry Billing was Mrs. Hibbert's nephew! Almost certainly, now, he was also her murderer. But even with this new knowledge, Chudd found that some questions remained unanswered. It still didn't explain why Mrs. Hibbert had given Peggy Dunkley a false reason for evicting her – or even why she'd evicted her at all, though Chudd thought he could perhaps speculate with reasonable intelligence about that. Similarly he thought he might now know why she'd had in mind to change her will.

But whether his speculation would be proved correct and whether the answers to these riddles would become finally revealed depended on one person alone, and that person was Terence Billing.

14

O F the numerous telephone calls which Chudd put through before once more making tracks for Bedford, the last one was to Mr. Dann.

"It's about Mrs. Hibbert's will, or rather her intention of altering it."

"Now, wait a minute, Chief Inspector," the solicitor broke in sharply, "I really must ask you to be more careful what you say. I am quite certain I have never told you that Mrs. Hibbert proposed to change her will, because I have no evidence of that fact."

"Perhaps I might explain the reason for my call," Chudd now broke in in his own turn. "And let me take it step by step.

About ten days before her death, Mrs. Hibbert wrote to you asking for an appointment."

"That is so."

"And the date finally fixed for her to come and see you was after her death?"

"Also correct."

"And it was definitely about her will that she wanted to see you?"

"So she mentioned on the telephone."

"A will which had been made six years before?"

"Yes, in nineteen sixty."

"Now I know, Mr. Dann, you have no evidence that she was proposing to change it, but nevertheless wasn't that your impression?"

There was a significant pause before the solicitor answered, and when he did so his words had a fragile sound.

"Ye-es, I believe that was my impression." Hastily he added, "But you realise that I couldn't possibly support that in a court of law."

"No, quite. It's only your impression I'm anxious to obtain, as it could be of great assistance to me in arriving at a conclusion about a certain matter."

"Then I confirm that was my impression."

"Was it an impression that she definitely wanted to alter it?"

"Oh, really, Chief Inspector, how can I answer a question like that? You're asking me to recollect vocal nuances."

"Yes."

"Well, if I have to say something, I suppose it would be that my impression was that she hadn't definitely made up her mind to alter her will, but that it was something she might wish to do in certain circumstances."

"I'm most grateful, Mr. Dann. You've been a great help."

"But don't ask me to commit what I've just said to paper," the solicitor said anxiously.

"I won't," Chudd replied in a pacifying tone. "One final matter, does the name Billing mean anything to you?"

"In connection with what?"

"With Mrs. Hibbert?"

"No."

"Have you ever heard of Albert, Catherine or Terence Billing?"

"No. Who are they?"

"I'll be able to tell you shortly. Meanwhile, my thanks again."

Billing's expression was stern and unfriendly when he entered the room where Chudd and Sergeant Roberts were waiting for him. Police officers don't drive from London to Bedford twice in a single day without a good reason, and he gave the appearance of being ready for the coming show-down.

He sat down at Chudd's invitation and stared stonily at the two C.I.D. men. His escorting prison officer moved his own chair beside the door and looked bored. There were times when being nanny to a bunch of prisoners got him down and this was one of them. At least it wasn't as bad as court duty, when you could scarcely yawn without the judge glaring at you.

"I've found out that Mrs. Hibbert was your aunt," Chudd said in a conversational tone. "Do you admit it?"

Billing pressed his lips together and then rubbed the back of his hand across his mouth.

"Got a cigarette?"

Chudd glanced at Sergeant Roberts who handed him one and lit it. Billing inhaled deeply and allowed the smoke to come dribbling down his nostrils and from the corner of his mouth.

"O.K., so she was my aunt."

"I'm now obliged to caution you," Chudd said and rapidly paraphrased the rigmarole which the Judges' Rules required him to intone. "Did you murder her?"

Billing stared meditatively at the burning tip of his cigarette.

"It's a pity you've found out about her being my aunt. God knows how you did it, but it rather clinches things against me, doesn't it?" Chudd remained silent, and after a moment he went on. "I mean, there's not much point in trying to deny anything any longer. It's not that I want to make your job any easier, but I can't see a way out of this now." In a mocking tone, he added,

"Aunt Florence has her revenge after all." He glanced at Sergeant Roberts who was busily making notes. "Am I going too fast for you?"

"Don't worry about me," Roberts replied tartly.

"Would you like to tell me the whole story from the beginning?" Chudd asked.

Billing let out a weary sigh, "Might as well, I suppose, particularly as I didn't intend to kill her. It was sort of an accident. . . ."

"What about starting at the beginning?"

"Oh, yes, the beginning! Until the evening I went to her house I hadn't seen my aunt for twelve years, but once every so often, I'd drop her a line and that usually produced a couple of quid from her. Once it was a fiver, but that was near Christmas. Anyway, while I was in Borstal this last time, she wrote and suggested I should visit her when I came out. It was quite a long, friendly letter this one. She said I was her nearest relative in this country and she thought it was time I stopped wrecking my life and she'd be prepared to help me. It was mostly a ruddy lecture and I didn't much go for it. However, I replied and said I'd think about it, but I wouldn't make any promises. And I happened to mention when I was due for release." He paused and ground out his cigarette on the floor. "That was about two months ago or more, and I heard nothing further until a week before my release, when she wrote to me again."

"Do you still have the letter?"

"No, I destroyed them all. Letters are dangerous things to hang on to in my sort of life."

"Yes, go on."

"Well, this last letter of hers came as something of a surprise because she actually suggested I should go and stay with her when I was released, while I was getting my bearings, as she put it. She even said she'd get rid of her lodger in the hope that I would take up her offer." He made a face of cynical resignation and went on, "She again repeated about my being her only surviving relative in England and how she was getting on in

172

years and had never had any children of her own. To be quite frank, I thought she was going a bit soft. Anyway, after my release, I spent a bit of time thinking about it."

"Did you reply to that letter?" Chudd broke in.

Billing shook his head. "No, I didn't want her to think I was proposing to be at her beck and call. However, I decided in the end that there wouldn't be any harm in looking her up, though I had no intention of staying in her house. But I thought I might at least collect another fiver if I played my cards aright. So I did call on her. It was about half past nine on the Friday night. Everything was a bit awkward at first, but after a while she started off about turning over a new leaf and she'd like to help me, and I kind of stalled and said I must have time to think and perhaps I'd emigrate to Canada. But when she said I could move in right away as she'd already got rid of her lodger, I told her 'no' and that I just couldn't see myself living there."

"Did she say anything about how she got rid of her lodger?"

"Yeah, I believe she did. She said she was a bossy school teacher and she'd had to tell her a lie because she'd have kicked up such a fuss if she'd known she was being thrown out for a Borstal boy. My aunt hinted that as she'd gone to so much trouble to get her out, I was really under an obligation to move in." He frowned in recollection of the episode. "That was what I was determined to avoid, *obligations*. Anyway, when she saw she couldn't persuade me, she said she'd nevertheless like to keep in closer touch than before and she again sang her song about going straight."

"Did she mention her will?"

Billing looked at Chudd sharply. "Do you mean she's left me something?"

"No, she hasn't done that," Chudd replied. It seemed an unnecessary cruelty to add, however, that this might well have been this prospect if he had played his cards differently.

"What happened next?"

"She went out of the room to see to her cat which was making noises in the kitchen. While she was away, I happened to notice her handbag and I was just having a dekko inside when she suddenly came back into the room again. Then she really went for me, said she was sorry she'd ever given me a second's thought, that I obviously had a rotten streak and the sooner I was back behind bars the better. I got pretty mad as she went on and I told her to shut up, but she wouldn't so I slapped her one and she screamed and it was then it happened . . . After she was dead I carried her body upstairs and put it beneath the bed. And then I got out as quickly as I could."

"Did you take anything?"

"Bit of money."

"Anything else?"

"Oh, you mean the key! It was on the table in the hall. You never know with keys, they sometimes come in useful." His gaze met Chudd's. "And that's about the lot."

"You haven't mentioned Sherbrook?"

"Oh, him! I met him like I've already told you."

"And you related to him how you'd killed your aunt."

"I told him bits and pieces in conversation like. We were sort of birds of a feather. But I didn't mention she was my aunt." His lip curled. "You should have seen his face when I was telling him. I might have been showing him dirty pictures."

"And after he'd confessed to your murder, I take it you decided to push your luck a bit farther and plant the key in his cell."

"It seemed a good idea," Billing said casually. "And it wasn't very difficult after that to fix things so that our cells would be searched. I just dropped a word into grasser Doyle's ear."

For several seconds Chudd contemplated the floor between his feet, while Billing watched him. On reflection, he was satisfied he now had the answers to all that had been puzzling him for so long. At last, the case made sense, the two halves did belong together after all.

Looking up, he said, "You'll be charged with the murder, of course."

"Well, you know it all now. I'm sorry about the old girl's

death in a way, not that I have very much to thank her for. Her offer of help came about fifteen years too late."

As they drove back to London, Chudd viewed without enthusiasm the work which lay ahead of him. Solving a case was far from the end of the matter, and in this particular one there was a considerable amount of unscrambling to be done. And so his sense of satisfaction was mitigated by the prospect of all the paper work yet to be undertaken, the conferences to be attended and the court hearings to be endured.

And when that was all over, the growing pile of number one dockets would still be waiting and other crimes would by then have been committed.

It was often difficult to remain patient and fair-minded under the pressures to which they were subjected, but Chudd hoped he would never lose sight of the importance of so being.

"Pity the bastard can't be hanged," Sergeant Roberts remarked suddenly, giving vent to his own line of thought.

Chudd was silent for a moment, then taking his pipe from his mouth and gazing at it with a rapt expression, he said quietly, "I'm glad he can't be."

www.ingramcontent.com/pod-product-compliance
Ingram Content Group UK Ltd.
Pitfield, Milton Keynes, MK11 3LW, UK
UKHW022310280225
455674UK00004B/246